Grace McCleen

Grace McCleen's first novel, *The Land of Decoration*, was published in 2012 and was awarded the Desmond Elliott Prize for the best first novel of the year. It was also chosen for Richard & Judy's Book Club and won her the Betty Trask Prize in 2013. Her second novel, *The Professor of Poetry*, was published by Sceptre in 2013 and was shortlisted for the Encore Award. She read English at the University of Oxford and has an MA from York, and currently lives in London. *The Offering* is her third novel and was longlisted for the Baileys Women's Prize for Fiction 2015.

'Setting aside the verve and dark lyricism of its prose, and the keenness of observation (especially of the natural world), what shines through is a real understanding, not only of what it is to be mentally ill, but also of the everyday dynamics of mental health institutions and the power struggles that underlie the psychiatric profession . . . It is also keenly observant of the ways in which men play God and of the power of the oppressed imagination to create an inhabitable world, even under near-intolerable conditions.'
John Burnside, *Guardian*

'That McCleen is a writer of exceptional gifts is beyond doubt. Her prose can soar in moments of breathtaking beauty, most particularly when she turns a poet's eye on the landscape . . . she writes equally viscerally about her narrator's emotional terrain, depicting claustrophobia, shame and terror so painfully it makes your skin itch'
Stephanie Merritt, *Observer*

'Grace McCleen's talent for description, especially when portraying the natural world, is quite exquisite.'
Carol Midgley, *The Times*

'A bold, mature, terribly sad novel'
Claire Allfree, *Daily Mail*

'Immersed in classic literature, especially at its loneliest and most febrile, it is fascinating to read Madeline bring these intellectual and imaginative resources to bear on questions she appears to lack the resources to settle. Huge questions, of faith, time, reality, individual responsibility and human sexuality are given pained and peculiar answers . . . Impressive, a plausible and moving account of mental illness'
Sam Kitchener, *Daily Telegraph*

Grace McCleen
The Offering

SCEPTRE

First published in Great Britain in 2015 by Sceptre
An imprint of Hodder & Stoughton
An Hachette UK company

First published in paperback in 2015

1

A CIP catalogue record for this title is available from the British Library

ISBN 9781444770025

Typeset in Sabon MT 12/14pt by Palimpsest Book Production Limited,
Falkirk, Stirlingshire

Printed and bound by CPI Group (UK) Ltd, Croydon, CR0 4YY

Hodder & Stoughton policy is to use papers that are natural, renewable
and recyclable products and made from wood grown in sustainable
forests. The logging and manufacturing processes are expected to
conform to the environmental regulations of the country of origin.

Hodder & Stoughton Ltd
Carmelite House
50 Victoria Embankment
London EC4Y 0DZ

www.sceptrebooks.com

This book is dedicated to Ella

Lethe: a river in Hades whose water, when drunk, made the souls of the dead forget their life on earth.

PROLOGUE

*

Lethem Park Mental Infirmary
June 2010

The Quiet Room

There has been a great deal of talk here recently about an event concerning myself and Dr Lucas, which took place from what I can gather in the Platnauer Room some two weeks ago. I presently find myself in the Quiet Room while Dr Hudson, who has taken over my care in Dr Lucas's absence, devises an appropriate plan. I said to Dr Hudson: 'I do hope that whatever happened will not prevent my release from Lethem Park, something Dr Lucas talked about on many occasions.'

That was when Dr Hudson stared at me.

People have been staring at me a great deal lately. I have become something of a celebrity. I am sure you could ask anyone on this ward who I was and they would say: 'That's Madeline Adamson.' Then they would stare at me some more. Their eyes used to pass over me as if I were a chair or a cabinet; now they widen and darken, as if the chair had sprouted arms and legs, as if its arms had reached up to the fluorescent light like branches craving alms of the sun, and its legs twisted, tuber-like, into the carpet.

This attention neither excites nor disturbs me. In fact, I cannot remember a time when I felt so peaceful. What is more, I am sure it has nothing to do with the cocktail of medication I have been prescribed; there have been periods before when I have been sedated and I was far from peaceful although temporarily stupefied. Now, however, I find I am contented to drift from one moment to the next and if several hours pass in which I have done nothing other than consider my hands in my lap or the birds beyond the window, it does not matter. I celebrate time, I press it into my hands. I receive it like water in a desert, yet when it slips through my fingers I do not mind.

I think upon reflection this room should be called the Empty Room. It contains only a chair, a mattress and a sink. It is rather pleasant to occupy a room so unashamed of its own emptiness. Recently space has become pleasant to me; it lets in the light. For the past forty minutes or so I have been gazing at a block of sunlight high up on the opposite wall. The room is getting darker now but I do not move to switch on the light. They will switch it on soon enough. They will slide the panel across. They will say: 'You mustn't turn off the light.'

And I will say: 'Why?'

I have just caught sight of one of the younger nurses peering in at me through the window in the door. I smile at her but she slides the panel shut. I wonder what startled her. People have been behaving so mysteriously recently, even Margaret. She doesn't come into the room any further than she has to and seems almost anxious to leave. I am glad to say that in the last few days, presumably having observed that I am not exhibiting any signs of alarming behaviour, something of the old friendliness has developed between us again, though not perhaps the same degree of warmth.

I don't know, I can't read people any more. I can't see what's underneath. When I was a child I was a great reader. I looked for the message inked high in slow-turning clouds, the thing in the ground, in the air; there in the beat of the line. Now when I look for a sign I'm not quite so sure. Things cast long shadows, they threaten to gesture, but finally pull back, withholding revelation.

Lucas could not read me. I remember this much. Those who cannot read cannot see. I was raised to do both.

GENESIS

*

Lethem Park Mental Infirmary
January 2010

Beginning

The new doctor has taken an interest in my case. It has been gravely neglected, he says, much misunderstood. He has a plan. If I follow it he anticipates good results. But let me describe him.

He roared into a parking space beneath the startled horse-chestnut trees two weeks ago in a low-slung sports car. A door like a wing rose up. Two lucent brogues appeared on the gravel. The door swung down, the brogues advanced. I watched it all from my window.

His name is Dr S. Lucas, he is over six feet tall, speaks with a booming voice and has a laugh that rings down corridors. He has blue-black hair that is swept straight back from his brow and piercing black eyes. Staff and patients part before this person like the waters of the Red Sea, from which he emerges without a drop adhering to his sheeny suit. I have seen more than one of the younger nurses blush in his presence.

I met him on Friday. He was sorting papers at the desk when I knocked at the Platnauer Room and he came towards me, extending his hand. 'Madeline,' he said. 'Come and take a seat.' It was as if he had been waiting to meet me for ever.

The room smelt of emulsion and aftershave. I saw it had been renovated. A table lamp cast a note of sophisticated intimacy over the new carpet, leather upholstery and gilt-framed photographs of young children and wife, smiling Colgate smiles. On the desk was an iPad, notebook and bouquet of freshly sharpened pencils. A vase of white irises stood on the sideboard. The sight of them made me uneasy.

'You like the flowers?' He was looking at me enquiringly.

'Yes,' I said, but in truth the smell (or was I imagining that?) was making me giddy.

'I believe in bringing nature indoors,' he said. 'We are only just beginning to realize the therapeutic benefits of being in nature.' He launched himself back into the leather rotating chair and flipped open a brown folder. 'So, how are you?' He flicked through the papers in the folder, which presumably concerned myself.

I considered this, then replied: 'I don't know. I've been here too long to know things like that.'

He smiled slightly as if I had made a joke, though that was not my intention. He said: 'Yes, twenty years is a fair stretch by anyone's standards.'

'Twenty-one,' I said.

'Sorry, twenty-one. You've been round the mulberry bush, haven't you?'

He was referring no doubt to the plethora of therapies I have undergone since my admission at the age of fourteen, suffering from a depression (so they deemed it) that made normal functioning impossible, as well as periodic episodes of violent psychosis – 'psychotic breaks', the doctors call them – in which I lose consciousness and, apparently, my identity, and when I re-enter my body have no recollection of anything I have said or done. Thanks to medication, they occur now only once or twice a year.

'And yet,' he said, 'in spite of the attention your case has received, I believe the doctors who treated you have been misguided. We are not dealing with a breakdown here, bipolarity, hysteria or even catatonia; it was an *event* that brought you here; something happened the night you ran away. When the police found you, you were dishevelled, incoherent. Over the next few weeks you stopped speaking, eating and sleeping.'

He leant back in the seat, the black leather creaking appreciatively. 'I'm writing a seminal paper on amnesia's long-term effects, Madeline. I think you're suffering from dissociative amnesia. Something happened that was too traumatic for your mind to process. So it effectively erased it. Your current illness is symptomatic of such repression. Do you remember anything at all about that night?'

'No.'

'Do you feel the same person as that teenage girl?'

'No . . .'

'You feel different?'

'I don't feel anything at all.'

'You don't feel connected to the person you were then.'

'Yes.'

'So who are you now?'

I considered this for a moment. 'Nobody,' I said.

He nodded, then said: 'Madeline, with your consent I'd like to hypnotize you. Despite the delay of adequate treatment, I think rehabilitation is a real possibility.'

A moment passed. I said: 'I'm sorry?'

'Rehabilitation. I know the idea must seem unusual to you after all this time.'

I felt a surge, as if I had taken a leap off the edge of something and been borne up. The sensation was painful in its intensity.

I said: 'You won't find anything.'

'We'll see. The only problem is that since so much time has passed we don't have much to go on. There are no eyewitness statements, just the police reports, which I've looked over. Your father and mother have passed away?'

I nodded.

He took a pencil from a pot and began to sharpen it in a machine at the side of his desk. Presently he inspected the point and, apparently satisfied, opened the notebook. Then he asked me to tell him how it began, 'the trouble', he called it, the year I was thirteen; the autumn, the winter, the summer and spring. He said he wanted to know how it was before things went wrong, and how they went wrong, and how it felt.

He said: 'Nothing is too bad to be talked about, Madeline.' I don't know why he said that.

'It's a long time ago,' I said.

I was surprised to find that Dr Lucas, in spite of the flowers, in spite of the aftershave, has a fine, steady gaze. 'I think you can remember,' he said.

I said: 'I need a drink.'

He allowed me to pour myself one from the water-cooler. When I sat down again he was still waiting. I made him wait while I drank, then I crushed the plastic cup and sat there a moment looking at it.

'I've been through all this a dozen times with a dozen doctors!' I said.

'And none of them looking in the right place,' he said. He raised his eyebrows. 'Madeline,' he said softly. 'I can help you.'

Yes, I thought – and write that paper on amnesia.

He got up. 'Have you heard of fugue, Madeline?' I could no longer see him without turning my head, which I was disinclined to do, unwilling to give anything he did more attention than was absolutely necessary. 'Fugue is a loss of identity, usually coupled with flight from one's normal environment,' he was saying. 'In your case you're still running.'

I fixed my eyes on the irises. The longer I watched them, the more sure I became that they were moving slightly, though I suppose they could not have, for there was no draught.

He came back to the desk and he said: 'Look at me.'

With some difficulty I did so. 'Do you want to stay here the rest of your life?'

Seeing as most of my remembered life had been spent here, it was not easy to say.

'Let's start somewhere,' he said. 'Anywhere. We can layer on the rest as the mind gives way.'

I put my head in my hands and leant forwards. I was trying to think how to explain what I knew. I felt my way back, but the threads were knotted. If I pulled here, a mass bunched there; I separated one strand, only for the others to tangle. I thought it must surely have begun the day I went down to the river. But then I thought it began the day Father came home without work. Then I thought perhaps it really began the day we arrived at the farm, rumbled up the track, opened the gate and stood looking around as if we had found ourselves in some enchanted land and didn't care to find the way out again.

All these years, there have been things I cannot remember, blanks where the colours had faded or the lines had been wiped out, and there have been others that darkened even as I watched, like photographic paper left too long in developing fluid.

But I could draw you a map, accurate to the metre, of the track and the house and the sheds and the courtyard, the sheep-dip and the garden, the pine tree and stream, the brambles, the dairy, the barn. I could tell you that the house stood facing east, that the sun rose over the dairy and set over the barn, and that from my bedroom you could see the country around for more than sixty miles, as far as the blue mountains on clear days. But you could not see the garden, though it encircled the house on three sides like a snake.

I could tell you about the moon as it rose through the branches of the pine tree, describe the feel of the stair banisters, the sound when my bedroom window opened, the precise shape of the crack in the kitchen ceiling that appeared the day my father hit his head on the beam. I could tell you that the cobbles in the courtyard were a sundial if you looked down from above, with the front door standing at number twelve. That there was a rust-coloured line running from the hole in a granite millstone that stood beside the front door, and that maybe *this* was where everything began, because the stone reminded me of an altar and the rust of blood.

The sky beyond the windows was heavy with rain. I could see the storm coming over the horse-chestnut trees, rolling faster than a person could run. I wanted to smell that air, be beneath those clouds, feel the dark spirit forms of the trees cover me.

I said: 'It began with a book.'

'A book?' He picked up his pencil.

'Yes.'

'What sort of a book?'

'A bible.'

'Whose?'

'My father's.'

'Go on.'

'What do you want to know?'

'What was the bible like?'

'Big.'

'Anything else?'

'Old.'

'Yes . . .'

'Inside the front cover there was a picture.'

'What of?'

'A garden.'

The Garden in the Book

My father was a minister of God. He believed this world was a template of another, a stained-glass window in which we could see things to come, and we lived accordingly, looking for signs, living by shadows, moment by revelatory moment. In the evenings my father read from a large bible. My mother and I listened, hearing the pattern and keeping the time, sitting either side of him, for the bible was too old to handle and too heavy to hold. A red bookmark forked like a tongue hung from the centre of the bible and the edges shone dimly with greening gold-leaf. Mildew had peppered the pages, and time had yellowed and warped each one so that they resembled the waters of a lake, perpetually rippling away from itself towards the shore. The smell of the bible I remember most keenly. It was, after the cantankerous creak of the spine, its most evocative aspect: fusty, acrid, furtive; suggestive of things ravaged yet fecund with time.

I mention this book because its fate seemed to presage our own; I mention it also because in the front of it there was a picture. There were many others throughout in black and white but there was only one coloured plate and this was at the beginning. It was the best-preserved part of the book because of two greaseproof pages between which it curtained itself off as exclusively as the Most Holy. When lifted, the veils revealed a page thicker than the rest and shiny. The illustration was of a garden, and its hues were jewelled, as if in their newly created state the trees, fruits and animals were at the apogee of saturation.

It was curious in the garden. It wasn't quite heaven and it wasn't quite earth. Vivid fruits and exotic flowers grew there; fountains of water showered the foliage and shape-shifters lurked within it: chameleons, frogs, birds, butterflies. Globes that resembled small planets hung from the boughs of trees, and fruits and flowers glowed alike with an unnatural luminescence as if illuminated from within. The vegetation itself gave off a greenish phosphorescence that to my young mind resembled the light emanating from Heavenly Jerusalem. But in the darker colours lay something irredeemably earthy. There was a harmony in the way the scene arranged itself that suggested a theatre, each view giving on to a fainter one, and that on to a fainter one still, till the whole regressed into a ghostly vista of infinite depth like theatrical flats on a stage – yet the creepers and canopies cavorted in lusty confusion, the trees reaching sinuous fingers (frantically, ecstatically: I never could decide) towards the viewer.

Where the light did not reach, it was shady. It was shadiest of all in the bowers. In the darkest one of them all, you could make out a man and a woman. This was indeed what they were, but to begin with all you could make out was the paleness of their skin, an absence of colour in a scene that was saturated, so that at first glance they resembled phantoms, a place where the printer had forgotten to lay ink, holes in the fabric of creation – two human-shaped holes, and beyond them nothing but light. The woman's head was bowed, the man's lifted. Both faces were curiously devoid of emotion, yet they held animal-skin mantles around themselves and huddled together as if they were shivering, or as if they too were aware of the shocking impression their nakedness made. Their faces were blank, yet they were turning away from the viewer, writhing, as if willing him or her to replace the greaseproof page – or perhaps turning away from something else, for behind them, in the centre of the garden, was a clearing and a tall tree with a snake in its branches, and in front, hanging upon nothing at all, a sword with a gleaming blade.

The most disturbing thing of all, whether owing to sympathetic or malevolent intent I could not decide, but made more disturbing by the void of the humans' own faces, was that the trees and flowers, animals and birds, all seemed imbued with an anthropomorphic life force – or, as I thought then, were conscious, as trees and flowers and creatures could not be. The trees (an unlikely assortment of deciduous and evergreen, together with various vines) craned their boughs over the humans as if whispering, their leaves skimmed their hair, tendrils fingered flesh. One creeper had coiled itself around the woman's left arm in a bracelet, another ensnared her partner's right foot. Birds cocked their heads sideways and watched avidly. One flew up, calling. A small horse-like creature pawed the air; a peacock spread his feathers in a full hand of petrol-green fright; a lion laughed, or appeared to; a dog lifted its head and howled; and a chimpanzee, whose forehead was creased as if by all-too-human anxiety, covered its mouth as if at some horror too great to be spoken.

When I was a child I thought it odd that the first thing the humans did after they sinned was to clothe themselves; after all, God knew what they looked like – and who else could they be hiding from?

'Why did they put clothes on?' I asked.

'So they would remember,' was the answer.

'That they had sinned?'

'Yes.'

'And then they left the garden and wandered the earth?'

'Yes.'

'Why did they do that?'

I was told: 'So they wouldn't forget.'

Undead

How to describe Lethem Park? This is not easy.

I suppose I could start by saying that Lethem Park is a maze of endless, slightly sloping corridors surrounded by acres of mature parkland. It was built to house wounded soldiers in the Second World War and an air of sickness still hangs about its grey passageways, whose sorry pot plants, automated pumps of air-freshener and Impressionist artwork cannot quite counterbalance their humming sterility. There is a pharmacy, a church, a shop, a large grassy area where we may graze if supervised, encircled by a twelve-foot electric fence; animals jump fences but humans seem to like them. I suppose without them there would be nothing to tell them who they are, what food to eat, what clothes to wear or what they should look like – and humans *like* to be told; they are obedient creatures. Of course none of us here cares much about those things so perhaps it is just as well we are fenced off. If we weren't, what would there be to tell where us crazy people end and the rest of the world begins?

Naturally enough, the word 'crazy' sounds exciting, but generally life at Lethem Park is a peaceful affair. So peaceful, in fact, that observing the progress along these corridors of various residents, the quiet mutterings and shamblings, the faces bleached of colour, eyes glazed, you would be forgiven for thinking that many of us had shuffled off this mortal coil for good. If death is a sleep, then this is a place of the deathlike, of sleepwalkers and ghosts; there is the odd wail, the occasional rattling of a chain, but it is soon forgotten; we have lost the knack of remembering, you see; we have very few markers of time past and present.

Sometimes, when passing time in the lounge, standing at the end of the landing, looking down at the horse-chestnut trees, I wonder whether I have slipped out of time altogether. Each day there is just enough change to show I am alive yet not enough to differentiate that day from the next. Life descends to a level of such minutiae – the challenges of casting off; of determining whether it will be fine tomorrow, whether Alice has been cheating at *Guess Who?*, of determining whether it will be curried lamb or cottage pie, the *Daily Mirror* or Miriam's scrapbook – that the monotony of each choice is matched only by the irrelevance of the decision.

Now, I of all people appreciate the principles behind peaceful activities – which I suppose was what the Occupational Therapy team at Lethem Park had in mind when they decreed that patients' days be interspersed with Coffee'n'Chill, Choc'n'Chill, mid-afternoon 'Chill' and bedtime 'Chill', at which time, along with the compulsory tea, coffee or chocolate, a nurse arrives with a tray of coloured pills in plastic beakers that we take as we would a sweet or a biscuit, pretending to choose, pretending our names are not written on the side of the cups in permanent black marker – but it seems to me we are slightly missing the point of relaxation; that many of us, far from being 'chilled', are on the verge of apoplexy.

Once, in the Occupational Therapy room, in my first couple of years here, I was attempting to busy myself by drawing with chalk a bowl of artificial flowers, when I suddenly became convinced that I was dreaming. I got up, weeping, and ran down the corridor, looking for an exit, some thinner place where the fabric would burst if pressed hard enough, some chink through which I could tumble out of this amniotic sac and be birthed again somewhere else. That presupposes an outside, I suppose, an end; something different to this – a 'that'; something else, something other.

This morning I am sitting in one of the high-backed chairs in the lounge, gripping *Wuthering Heights*, unable to raise it from my lap because of nausea, unable to read because my eyes will not convert the markings on the page into thoughts, unable to speak because of an exhaustion too profound for words. This is a bad day. In a while, having done my hour here, I will ask if I can go and lie down. Someone will bring the wheelchair and take me to my room where I will get into bed (though I will not sleep) till dinnertime. Whereupon I will sit up, try to eat something, lie down again and wait for bedtime (a term itself meaningless, so much of my time being spent in bed). Upon which, too sick to sleep, I will toss until morning. Whereupon, too sick to rise, I will begin another day. On very bad days I cannot wake up at all; sleep is a pit I fall into and clamber out of, again and again.

It is sunny this afternoon but cold. All day Lethem Park has been slumbering beneath a thick layer of frost. Birds peck frantically at the ground; trees creak; what leaves remain shiver, I imagine. For we are unaware of these struggles here, cocooned as we are in our gauze of central heating, drugs, fitted carpet. With the humming of the boiler, we cannot hear the stillness that has wrapped the world beyond the window-pane. The seasons pass by like pictures in a book thumbed too quickly.

I pressed my fingers through the bars of the long window by the exercise bike on the landing today, trying to feel the cold, and could not; like the souls it encases, the window is double-glazed. Yet I live for the moments when the natural world interacts with my own, for the sound of rain on glass, wind in the guttering, the smell of pine needles in the lounge at Christmas, the feel of a butterfly's wings against my palm; for those moments when I can touch something beyond the boundaries of this world.

Once, during a storm, I got as far as the fence. We were walking back from the post office, Robyn and Brendan and Margaret and I, with our weekly ration of sweets. The clouds that day reminded me of those at the farm when the apples turned bad and the lightning struck the chimney. They made my skin crackle and my hair stand on end. We were turning into the courtyard when I broke rank and began running towards the fence. As I began to run the heavens opened. Air seared my lungs, the gale pummelled me. I could taste iron and sulphur and soil; I was elbows and knees, a child in dungarees, my heart in my cheeks and my lips and my eyes. And for the rest of that day, after Margaret's remonstrations, after the visit to the Platnauer Room – ('How did you manage it?' they asked. 'Some days you can't even walk to the lounge'; I wanted to, I said. I do not want to walk to the lounge) – after the removal of privileges, the talk about trust and responsibility, I felt it still, a gentle throbbing, not unlike, I imagine, a virgin must feel after her deflowering; a call to further forays. They did not let me go out again after that. Margaret seemed to take it even harder than I did. Why did I do it, she asked: I, who enjoyed walks more than anyone? Didn't I think there would be consequences? I told her that at that moment I was not thinking of anything at all.

I sometimes imagine taking these brothers and sisters of mine back to the farm. We would cram our mouths with wild strawberries, run naked through the long grass, bathe in the river and play in the wood. We would sleep beneath the sky, dew drenching our bodies, aching in cold and roasting in heat. I would ask the land to refine us, separate us from ourselves, sift the good from the dross and the wheat from the chaff, as it does for each of its children, the stones and the creatures and trees. First pleasure, then pain, which are one and the same, until we became impermeable as stones, as light as air, no more than process, an event, infinitely transferable. Undead. Like the soil under our feet.

I would ask the land for release.

At this moment the park as seen from the garden doors resembles a painting by Turner. A haze of golden moisture blurs the horse-chestnut trees and the spaces between until there is nothing left but a sea of light interspersed by gigantic shadows. It is, I suppose, quite beautiful.

It is now the time of our mid-afternoon 'Chill'. We have just been medicated. Pam, mousy hair short as a marine's, huge-shouldered in her pink mohair jumper, is completing a jigsaw on the carpet in a pool of sunlight, laying the pieces in patterns of her own. Robyn – blue-veined, white-skinned, fragile as a bird, hair so fine I can see the skull gleaming through it – is moaning, a meaningless sound we would miss if it stopped. Eugene – rotund, ruddy, blond, sprinkled with eczema – is rubbing his groin with sausage fingers in an abstracted but vigorous way. Miriam is watching television, her eyes half closed and her mouth open, her tongue lolling loosely on her lower lip as if she has just stopped breastfeeding. Sue is reading a magazine, though not really reading it, I think, only passing the time. Pete the male nurse is playing snakes and ladders with Mary, and Margaret is knitting, her large hands almost obscuring the article she is making, which from what I can make out is white.

As for Brendan, he is sitting on the floor, fingers in his ears, bent over *The Cosmological Principle*; page fifty-nine, no doubt, though it may be page sixty. His arms are extended like two small wings and I wonder, as I have wondered many times before, how he manages to keep them raised so long.

I watch him read and rock till he comes to the end of the page, then stop. To turn over he must remove one finger from his ear. He sits thinking, jerks his head towards the book, then his elbow. He groans loudly, half rises and sits down again.

Margaret says: 'All right, Brendan?'

He begins rocking again. After another few agonized minutes he removes his finger from his ear for a split second before reinserting it, shaking his head vigorously as if to say: 'That wasn't a good idea at all.' Now he gets up and walks around the book with his tiny shuffling steps, his skeletal limbs resembling those of a mantis, making small movements towards the book as if it were a hot coal he must pick up without gloves. Then the desire to turn the page and the horror of doing so finally confront one another and he stands, prancing on the tips of his toes, his face twisted into a paroxysm of terror for a few seconds, before darting at the book and turning the page at the last moment. Once he has done so, his face fills with wonder and relief; he sits down and shuffles forward on his crossed legs, bending so far over the book you would think it would be impossible for him to read at all; but he is reading, his head is moving back and forth, and presently he resumes rocking as well. There is a joyful light in his eyes. The light will last until he has reached the end of the page, at which point they will once again cloud with terror.

Brendan refused his lunch again today. He is more twitchy than usual. I suspect it is all to do with the arrival of Dr Lucas; Brendan is our weathervane, our thermometer, our canary in the mineshaft. Any slight alteration, he registers first. I wonder whether the doctor has made changes to his treatment too or whether he is just responding to the general alterations Dr Lucas has made.

Of which there are many. No one is to be exempted from the dining room any more unless they are physically ill;

Sue and Margaret are no longer supposed to touch us unless it is to restrain; a penalty system has been introduced with a board in the lounge, on which the nurses must make black marks if we are disobedient and red marks if we are good (Brendan has three black marks against his name, I have one); only those who accrue no black marks are allowed to go to the shop every Saturday (this does not include me because I forfeited my right to go to the shop when I ran to the fence); dinner is now to be eaten at a single sitting by multiple wards at once; and last, but perhaps most importantly, Dr Lucas has cut our meeting time with the panel every third Wednesday.

I was astonished when I heard of this: appearing before the panel is our opportunity to voice our concerns with the board of doctors. Those patients who cannot voice their own concerns are represented by a nurse. Each of us used to get half an hour and though I always had reservations about how effective it was, as even then the doctors did most of the talking, at least it gave me the illusion I mattered; that in theory, at least, I could contribute to my own treatment.

'What do we do now?' I asked Margaret. 'Who do we go to if we are worried about something?'

'Dr Lucas,' she said.

'But he is the one devising our treatment anyway,' I said. 'Can't we speak to one of the other doctors?' We looked at each other.

'Apparently not,' she said.

She seemed worried. What will things be like months from now, for this is only the beginning? I wondered. And then the concept of a beginning, like that of an end, loses all credibility. Here at Lethem Park it can never be other than Now.

It is for this reason that if you asked me to tell you what Lethem Park is really like, I would not describe my fellow inmates, our everyday activities, our treatment or the doctors. I would describe the building itself. Mystics know that the visible is a husk from which the invisible, if attended to hard enough, can be unearthed. I know this to be true: the spiritual character of a place, and a person, can be known through its physical surface. Or am I deluding myself, existing as I do on a shirred margin between sanity and madness, truth and illusion, fiction and fact? In any case, in my attempt to communicate to you what this place is really like, I would tell you about the light: stark blue, insane yellow, ghoulish orange; fluorescent; man-made without exception. I would explain that even things that could be made of natural materials here – pillows, blankets, knives and forks – are synthetic. I would say that there are very few shadows, very few corners, very few places where darkness is permitted to exist; I would say that the light is excoriating, a lance to which we are the boil, and that beneath such light we appear sorry creatures indeed.

I would say that the walls and floors are perfectly uniform, and whichever floor, whichever wall you encounter will tell you nothing. The walls are cool, their surfaces regular; you would not think anything so even could continue for such distances. The walls are pale green and sheeny. Rails run along them, sloping or rising gently at intervals. And the rails, like the walls – like the floors – appear to be interminable. They converge at points that widen as you draw near, that promise arrival, only to reveal further vortices, further distances, further vanishing points. Every so often there is a picture, framed in brown wood, no matter the subject or the style. Oddly, the pictures themselves are all explosions of some kind, the colours primary, vibrant, the compositions overblown and dramatic, usually flowers or fruit. Unfortunately the pictures not only fail to enliven, but their ghastliness serves only to emphasize the surrounding pallor, like blusher on a corpse.

I have spent days studying the walls, I have set my eye parallel to their surface and run my hand over their planes, scouring them for fissures, discrepancies, flaws of any sort – I do not know why this matters so much – and when I found even the slightest crack, tears of joy would spring to my eyes and I wanted to run and fetch someone, I wanted to draw a circle around the thing so it could not be lost, to frame it, erect a little grotto there, kneel in gratitude. In fact the only real singularity we know, the only end-point in this world of deferrals, is that which lies at the end of the long corridor: Block 'H'. Block 'H' is the undiscovered country from whose bourn no traveller returns. Or at least, no one has returned since I have been here.

To describe Lethem Park, then, I would tell you about surfaces and the interstices between them. I would describe the doors, the hinges of the doors, the bolts of the hinges. These things have come to mean more to me than people. I am a student of surfaces, I seek footholds in traces, animation in shades, intent in implacable geometry, meaning in the intractability of metal and concrete and stone. A tree, a scrap of bark would be braille to my blindness, balm to my skin. But then I remember that I wept at the foot of a tree and knelt in a bare field; I remember that meaning is a myth, a bedtime story told to young children who are afraid of the dark.

I am not afraid of darkness but of light. My terror is not black but white. But it doesn't matter now. All opposites fail to signify. There is nothing beneath the veil, below the surface, beyond the window, however beautiful the day may appear to be.

The Light

He sends for me again today. He says: 'I want to fill you in on what will happen when we begin hypnotherapy.'

'How are you going to do it?' I say, not wanting to seem interested but needing to know nonetheless.

'With a light.' He opens a drawer and takes out something like a pen with a white light at the end that appears when he clicks it.

'What do I do?'

'Follow the light.'

'Like the Israelites,' I say.

'I'm sorry?'

'Nothing.'

'We'll be using counting,' he says.

'Will I be able to stop if I want to?' I say.

'Of course. You're in the driving seat, Madeline. In any case, I shouldn't worry; some of my patients actually enjoy being hypnotized.'

He leans back in the chair, bobbing a little. 'Now, in addition to the hypnotherapy I'm going to provide you with some new strategies to target your symptoms head-on.'

He hands me four sheets of paper. The first reads: 'Lie or sit in a comfortable position. Breathe in for a count of ten through your nose . . .' The second begins: 'Imagine you are floating in a warm place . . .' The third: 'Lie on your back with your legs and arms . . .' The fourth is a table with numerous boxes running along the top. The first box says: 'Challenges to Initial Thoughts'.

'Let's run through the table,' he says. 'Okay: you feel some anxiety following a session. First of all, "Describe the Situation".'

'Describe the situation . . .?'

'Yes. For example: "In my room". It doesn't have to be lengthy, but it gives us helpful biofeedback from which to map patterns. Then: "First Thoughts about the Situation", such as "anxious about beginning new therapy".'

I scan the rest of the sheet. 'Then: "Feelings as a Result of Initial Thoughts"?'

'Exactly, then: "Challenges to Initial Thoughts".'

'Then: "Feelings after Challenges"?'

'Great!' he says. 'You get the picture. It's called Cognitive Behavioural Therapy – CBT. See how you go with it; even a five per cent improvement in negative thoughts is valuable.'

He produces a fifth sheet, a timetable. 'Graded Exercise,' he says. 'This illness of yours has to be targeted and targeted hard.'

'Eight-thirty: get up,' I read. 'Eight-fifty: stretches. Nine-ten: breakfast. Nine-thirty: breathing and relaxation.' I lower it and look at him. Then, as he gestures for me to continue reading, I resume.

'Ten o'clock: lie down for half an hour. Eleven o'clock: more stretches. One o'clock: lunch. Walk along the corridor. Two o'clock: Occupational Therapy. Three o'clock: snack, breathing exercises and relaxation. Four o'clock: sleep. Five o'clock: second walk along the corridor. Five-ten: stretches. Five-thirty: tea. Six o'clock: reading. Seven o'clock: social interaction in the lounge. Eight o'clock: thirty minutes' meditation. Nine o'clock: bed.'

I feel hot and sick. I say: 'I don't think I—'

But he is saying: 'Along with Cognitive Behavioural Therapy, Graded Exercise is the second most effective weapon we have in our arsenal against fatigue. Take a look at the last sheet.'

On a sixth sheet there is another table on which to note how many minutes I have been able to walk, how many books I have been able to lift, how many stretches I have completed. The sickness is increasing, winding its way up my arms and screwing itself into the base of my skull.

'I don't need this,' I say. I feel as if I am shouting but my voice is barely audible. 'It's not going to help.'

He leans back in the chair as if I have not spoken. 'I also want you to interact more,' he says. 'I'll expect you to visit the lounge at least once a day. It's no wonder you feel ill when you see people if you never do.'

'No,' I say. I feel dizzy. 'That isn't the reason.'

'Madeline, I know you may have reservations about this schedule but I'd really like you to give it a go, just for a few weeks. Is that acceptable? And report back to me then.'

I hold the sheets for a moment, trying to steady my hands. Then I fold them in half, fold them again, then fold them a third time.

'I know you're feeling some resistance; resistance is good, and it's understandable. But in order to achieve our objective we need to pass through it. And our objective is your rehabilitation, Madeline. I don't think it's harmful to remember that. Can I have your word you'll give this a go?'

Your objective, I think, but say nothing.

'Now,' he is saying, 'if it's all right I'd like to talk a little bit more about the time you moved to the island. You were thirteen, weren't you, when your parents bought the farm?'

I take a very deep breath and look towards the window.

'Were you thirteen, Madeline?'

I let the breath out. 'Yes.'

'And why did you move to the island?'

'My father wanted to.'

'But why did he want to move to an island?'

'He said the need was great.'

'The need?'

'For preachers.'

'Oh yes, your father was a Christian, wasn't he? Quite a zealous one.' He pauses a moment and I can hear his pencil scratching the paper. 'So there were no other Christians on the island?'

I shrug. 'My father had his own faith, a creed of one.'

'Or three,' he says, 'including you and your mother.'

'Yes.'

'So you moved in order to "spread the word".'

I nod and look down. 'The island was virgin territory,' I say.

'Presumably you were excited to be moving?'

I do not answer.

'Did you like the farm?'

'No,' I say.

'Oh. I thought I read—'

'"Like" isn't the word.' I find I am pleased to correct him.

'What word would you use?'

I think for a moment. 'Recognized.'

'What do you mean?'

'I thought I had seen it before.'

'Had you?'

'I don't know; not in everyday life. Maybe in a dream. There's a—' I stop, then, seeing it is too late, go on, angry at myself. 'A painting by Van Gogh . . .'

'Yes?'

'It looks like it a bit.'

'Looks like the farm?'

I nod, hot, still angry at myself.

'Really? What's it called?'

'I can't remember; *Sheds* or something ordinary like that. The place in the picture is almost identical to the drive that led up to the farm. The buildings too. I thought when

I saw it that it must have been painted by an artist standing in the lane . . .'

'Do you have a copy of this painting?'

'I've got a postcard of it in my room.'

'Interesting.' He looks up. 'Did you know that Jung posited there was a collective consciousness in which images, certain aspects of things – "archetypes", he called them – become a common psychic property?' He peers at my file. 'You arrived at the farm on the 12th June and a little over a year later on the night of the 14th you made your way to the sea. You have no idea why.'

I shake my head, then nod, unsure which action best affirms his statement.

He looks at me from under his eyebrows. 'You don't remember why?'

'No.'

'But you have a recurring dream about it, don't you? What happens in the dream, Madeline?'

After a moment I say: 'I'm walking along a road, I can hear the sea. I can't walk properly.'

'I wonder why that is.'

'I don't know.'

'What time is it in the dream?'

'Early morning.'

I hear the sound of the pencil and wonder, not for the first time, why a man who has the best of modern technology at his disposal chooses such an outmoded method to write; does the physical activity of writing provide some hidden benefit? Do the movements of lead on paper, the sound of its scratching, the shapes that appear beneath his hand, in banishing the nothingness from which they arise, encourage other shapes to emerge, other sounds, other movements? From the shadows of his mind, perhaps? Does the fact that the letters lead ineluctably onwards (as one letter cannot help but suggest the next, and the next, and the next) permit some conclusion to be reached – or do they only spawn more of the same?

I am recalled by his voice. 'The state you were in when the police found you points quite strongly to the fact that you were traumatized. Your clothes were damp. You were dishevelled, visibly distressed.'

He inhales sharply as if about to speak, but instead considers me a moment, then says: 'So, you're walking along a road by the sea. And it's early morning. And you can't walk properly. Then what happens?'

'A police car pulls up. They ask me my name, make a phone call and take me back to the farm.'

'Your mother by this time is in a critical state.'

I feel a prick, disconcerting, but not entirely painful, like the scratch of a needle entering numbed flesh. 'Yes,' I say quietly.

He frowns. 'Madeline, you said you changed when you moved to the island; can you explain a bit more about that?'

'I don't remember saying that.'

'Well, it's here in the notes. Can you think of anything that made you feel different?'

'No. Not really.'

But he waits so long that at last I say: 'Perhaps I began noticing things.'

'Really? Such as?'

'Nothing – little things, about people, about the countryside.'

He leans back in the chair and frowns. 'Why do you think you lasted such a short time on the island? The notes say you ran out of money but your father must have known before he moved what it entailed.'

'We met with one disaster after another.'

'So it was just bad luck? Is that how it felt to you, as a child?'

'At the time—'

30

'Yes?'

I smile to show him how ludicrous I find such an idea now. 'At the time I thought God had withdrawn His protection from us.'

'Protection from . . .'

'The forces of darkness.'

'Really? Why would He do that?'

'Transgression,' I say. And then suddenly I am tired. 'I don't feel well, can we stop here?'

'We've nearly finished,' he says, 'but this is important, Madeline; transgression – on your part?'

'I don't know.'

'Are we talking about transgression as a family or by one member?'

'It wouldn't matter.'

'Do you think your parents also thought you were being punished?'

'I think my father did.'

Lucas writes this down and then he says: 'Do you remember feeling guilty about anything?'

I say: 'We're going to have to leave it here, I can't talk any more.' But it is as if I have said nothing at all.

'Guilt is one of the biggest suppressants of memory,' he is saying. 'Do you feel guilty about anything that happened then?'

'I've already told you,' I say, and I get up and stand, looking down at him. 'I'm not the person I was then.'

Then I walk to the door.

A Condition of Complete Simplicity

It has been said that the past is a foreign country. If that is true, then the present is merely a holding centre where this body waits until it is time to go back. This place is merely a wayside, somewhere to stop off. For many of my fellow patients the terminus turns out to be terminal, the tracks do not transport them onwards but narrow inevitably towards a vanishing point, which – while appearing to be deferred for years in a closed circuit, a loop of endless transmission, a living death – nevertheless, in time, turns out to be the final destination, the extremity, the end of the line.

For me the past ended the morning of my fourteenth birthday when police found me wandering the sea road of the island. When they took me home little less than an hour later, I had forgotten the events of the previous twelve hours. I do not consider the intervening twenty years to be 'past' in the conventional sense of the word. All that has happened is that my cells have succeeded in reproducing themselves, transforming a pre-pubertal body into this shameful spectacle of a woman.

It was raining the night I arrived here. My father came into my bedroom and picked me up in my blankets. He laid me in the back of the car. The world was a wash of leather and dark branches, hissing tyres and sliding lights. He took me into a foyer, draped in my blanket.

'My daughter,' he said, as if presenting a gift.

For the first few months I do not remember doing anything but staring straight ahead of me. The diagnosis was breakdown, unusual in one so young. What part the parents' religious beliefs played was unknown but in view of the fact that any mention of such matters greatly agitated the patient, further religious activities, despite the father's concern, were curtailed forthwith.

My father continued to visit me on weekends for several years until his death. We sat opposite each other in high-backed chairs in front of the garden doors that looked onto the horse-chestnut trees and a lawn whose proximity, yet encasement behind two inches of reinforced glass, simultaneously promised and mocked the possibility of closer contact. The room was full of people who dribbled, banged their heads and attempted to fit square plastic blocks into round plastic holes. If they were good (did not bang their heads too often, took their tablets, played their games quietly) they were permitted to walk on the lawn.

Father read on, in the interests of my eternal welfare, the marble cadences of Revelation punctuated by the occasional scream, moan and wrestling match as one or more of my fellow patients refused to take their medicine. It made little difference to him that I was incarcerated in an asylum for the insane. He had never paid too much attention to physical realities. He believed we were all merely waiting, that life was a series of moments significant only in that they brought us closer to the final one, at which time we would be transfigured, one and all, into something immaterial.

Interestingly, over the years that I have been here it has not escaped my notice that despite their personal difficulties – and sometimes when they have more than enough reason to despair – nearly every other patient is a believer of some sort. There is Mary the ex-nun, Eugene the Jesuit, Robyn, who cries bitterly every Sunday because she will have to wait a whole week to go to church again, and Brendan, who is an ardent physicist and born-again Christian. It has made me wonder whether faith pre-dates mental disturbance or is a result of it. The apostle Paul says that faith is the 'evident demonstration of realities though not yet beheld', a definition I am also aware comes close to describing psychosis, for behind both faith and delusion lies unshakeable belief. The bible refers to the disciples of God as babes, as children, children of light, children of the promise. The description is fitting because children trust.

I am thinking these things, not wanting to and trying to reach a shoebox. It lies at the back of the top shelf of my wardrobe and inside it are three things: a journal, a bible and a dog's collar with a red name barrel. The journal is bound with string, the dog collar red, the bible mildewy. The shoebox is behind my books. I pull out an armful and let them clatter to the floor around me, shielding my head with my arms. Then I reach again, holding onto the chair-back, and feel it: the lid. I replace the books and sit on the bed with my back to the door and the shoebox in my lap and I take a deep breath. I lift out the bible, the journal I glance at, the dog collar not at all.

It is a small bible, mass-produced. A name in the front is written in a juvenile hand. It is the same name as mine. I recognize the address, the optimism with which it was written, the emphatic bubbles over the 'i's, the tails of the 'y's bending back on themselves like cheeky upside-down grins. But I did not write it. I open the bible and begin to read but before many minutes I am falling. My child self liked the sensation. At the farm there were steps built into the dairy wall. I would dangle my foot from the top step and see how far I could bend my knee without losing my balance. The knowledge that the air would part and close behind me without a trace was a source of fascination. The sensation now is not so pleasurable. Indeed, for several minutes I cannot move at all.

'How are you feeling?'

I jump. Margaret has put her head around the door. I roll sideways, obscuring the bible.

'Need any tablets?'

'No.'

She sits down beside me, smelling of washing powder and disinfectant, and something else I never quite manage to identify that is softer, like skin, and rather fragile, like infants or old people. Margaret must be about fifty. She has thick wiry white hair that is always a little greasy at the roots, and though parted on the side sticks up at the back. She has the sort of body that could never be feminine – the shoulders are too hefty, the ankles, the hands – but it makes me feel safer than anything else I know. Her face could never be pretty either, her jaw is too strong, her nose too long, the lips thin and jutting, but it is the kindest face I have ever seen, apart from my mother's.

'So how d'it go?' she says in her broad country accent.

'He wants to hypnotize me,' I say. 'He thinks I've got dissociative amnesia.'

She raises her eyebrows. 'That's a new one.'

I smile. Then I stop smiling and hesitate before I speak again. 'He thinks I can be rehabilitated.'

Margaret looks frightened, and then I think she seems to brighten, and then I think she looks angry. 'Well,' she says finally, and her voice is firm but guarded. 'That's good news.'

For a moment neither of us speaks. Then she says in a deeper voice: 'What are you doing with that bible?'

I feel my cheeks blush. There is very little that can be hidden from Margaret. 'Seeing if I could read it,' I say.

She pulls it out. 'Want me to put this back?'

I nod.

She takes it from me with a long look and I hear her replace the lid of the box, stand on the chair and stow it behind the books. As she gets down I hear her tights slither against one another.

We are silent for a moment, then she says: 'You can go into the lounge if you want, they've all gone to church so it's pretty quiet.'

'Okay,' I say.

'Are you going to have dinner?'

'Do I have to?'

'A little bit.'

'Any suggestions?'

'The beef stroganoff's all right but steer clear of the apricot pudding and custard; Carol's cooking and she's not particular about lumps.'

I smile. 'Then just the beef, please.'

'She won't be pleased, you know; she always knows when someone's skipped her dessert.'

At the door she stops and looks back at me. 'No more reading. Promise?'

I nod.

She looks at me.

'I promise, Margaret,' I say.

The Road through the Pines

I am alone, the room is still. I feel great currents move above me. The world thickens and slows. I lie and watch the sky in the high window darken. Sleep comes and I am grateful.

I wake to earth beneath my cheek, the smell of salt and of rain. There is sand in the earth. Birds are sitting in the black boughs above me. I have been here before. I remember.

The birds are singing now and the sound scatters amongst the bushes. A sun is rising, winking over the sea. I can tell by the colour of the sky that the day will be hot. I get up and begin walking.

The sand dunes give on to a road that winds through the pine trees. I do not know where I am going, I do not know where I have come from.

I hear nothing but my footsteps and the waves on the shore. There is a pain in my chest that makes me stop and when I go on I feel very tired. I cannot tell whether this is how I normally walk. My feet make a scraping sound and will not obey me. They dangle from my legs, slowing me down. My clothes are clammy and cling to my body. My hands smell like iron, like the hole in the millwheel at the farm, where the rust ran and stained the granite in a brown line. The sun rose a little while ago. It spun itself out into skeins of light and the woods were still.

Sometimes a car or a truck passes and sometimes it doesn't. Sometimes someone in the car or the truck stares back at me. I see their faces get smaller and smaller. I suppose I must be getting smaller too. Just now something came scudding over, racing towards me too quickly for me to dodge. A shadow moves beside me and I hear moaning. Now I want to wake up.

A car with letters on it pulls up in front of me and a man and woman get out. The woman comes towards me. She says: 'Are you Madeline Adamson?'

She has a badge on her chest but I cannot read it.

She says more loudly: 'Are you Madeline Adamson?' I frown, then I nod. She says: 'Are you all right, Madeline? Where have you been? Has anyone hurt you?'

The man is talking on his radio. He says: 'We've got her. Yeah. Wandering along the Head.'

The shadow flashes across my mind again and I hear panting. The woman puts her hand on my arm and says: 'Steady,' but something rises up my throat, opens my mouth and spills at her feet. Orange liquid slips down the sides of her shiny black shoes.

Suddenly I turn and kneel on the back seat as we drive away and stare out of the rear windscreen at the woods and the road and mile after mile of waving grass on the dunes. I watch fiercely though my face aches so much I think the flesh must slide down from the bones. I look hard and try to fix it all in my mind.

The man says: 'Sit down now, there's a good girl,' but I don't. I watch till the sea is a blue scrap of paper, till the woods hide the dunes, and they too are lost in the curve of the road.

Going Out

Judgment Day has come. It is evening. The best time, Lucas says, to be hypnotized.

He swings around as I enter the Platnauer Room: sharp, bronzed, navy-suited. 'Madeline, how are we today?'

We? Are there two of me now? Or were there always? But no matter. He and I are on the same team apparently, in name at least, and we share the same goal.

I consider how to respond to his question: that I was too exhausted to get up before three, then sat in a chair, clutching the pieces of a jigsaw? That I have attempted more stretches and felt worse than ever? That for days I have been troubled by the dream and that his relaxation exercises have done nothing but trouble my already unsettled mind?

'Well, thank you.'

'Good, good!' He seems to be in even better spirits than the first time I saw him. 'Up you get.' He pats the couch.

I tell myself to ignore the pat and lower myself onto the couch while he busies himself at the side of the room. A High Priest preparing the instruments. And I am the first fruits, I suppose; the first in his experiment with amnesia, at any rate. To distract myself from this unhappy thought I look at the ceiling, automatically scouring it for marks, and as usual finding none. There is not one stain, one cobweb, one minute fissure or crack; all is pristine and unrecognizable. I wonder what is above the ceiling, in the space between it and the next floor. I try to imagine how dark it is there, how cold or how warm, but my thoughts remain fixed where they are.

Here is the light. He moves it to the left, then to the right. 'Can you see that comfortably?' he says. 'Good. Now keep following the light.'

Despite my best efforts, my chest is rising and falling quite dramatically.

'Nothing bad is going to happen to you, Madeline,' he says. 'Remember, you can come back whenever you want to.'

'How?' I say.

'Your subconscious will know. It doesn't need your conscious attention. We leave it at the helm every night when we sleep. Have you ever thought of that? It knows how to keep us safe.'

I consider telling him about the dream but do not.

'Now,' he is saying, 'I'd like you to follow the light and count backwards, slowly and clearly, from one hundred. Are you ready?'

Am I?

Why are you doing this? I ask myself. The answer comes immediately: to get out. Why do I want to get out? To go home. Where is home? I don't know. Then how will I know when I find it?

My heart begins hammering so hard I think I will have to get up, and then I remind myself that people make homes. Perhaps I could make one. It occurs to me that all this seems laughably childlike. But then that is Lucas's point, isn't it: I am an emotional child. I decide that, although what I want may be impossible, I would still like to try.

'Yes,' I say. 'I'm ready.'

'All right. In your own time . . .'

'Ninety-nine . . .'

'. . . ninety-eight . . .'

'. . . eighty-one . . .'

'. . . sixty-two . . .'

'. . . fifty-five . . .'
'. . . forty-four . . .'
'. . . thirty-six . . .'
'. . . twenty-six . . .'

The words are footsteps leading me back. There will soon be no words and no light. The words begin to blur and I begin to wander.

I turn up the track and push wide a gate to stand in a sun-drenched courtyard. Blue distance whispers around me. There is the garden, the gate shrouded in ivy. Here is the house. I step under the lintel and turn right into the kitchen.

'Nineteen . . .'
'. . . eighteen . . .'
'. . . seventeen . . .'
'. . . eighteen . . .'

'Where are you?' says a voice.

I make myself look around: there is the dog's basket in the corner, his shape still inside it; there are the boots by a woodstove, one toppled sideways; dried flowers hang from beams. In the corner, stairs lead upwards. I climb, slipping deeper.

'Eighteen . . .'
'. . . seventeen—'
'. . . sevent—'

It happens at the last moment. I go out.

My hand touches wood, a latch clicks upwards, a door opens. White light streams out.

The voice asks: 'Where are you?'

I say: 'I am home.'

EXODUS

*

Lethem Park Mental Infirmary
March 2010

Just So

My father was a minister of God; he was also a man in constant search of a home. This may seem strange, considering the Christian belief in the transience of all earthly resting places and our ultimate reunion with an immaterial one, but people who are idealistic are rarely satisfied with the fulfilment of their ideal in one dimension and yearn for the realization of it in every other.

Big hopes were laid upon the move to the island, however, because God had shown him, clearly, he said, that this was where we should go.

'What about work?' my mother said.

God would provide.

Where would we live?

We would rent somewhere until we could find a place to buy.

Why there, why the island?

People needed to hear the message, he said; it was virgin soil.

But there was another reason: my father disliked towns. He stood in the marketplace every Saturday, with his placard above him and my mother and me beside him (me a little behind, if I am honest), shouting about the downfall of civilization and the return to the bucolic, and the people surged around him like water. Whether it was their continued indifference or the strain placed on his nerves by working amid chimneys and traffic and streets, I remember the wistfulness with which I occasionally found him dwelling on that picture in the front of the large bible, and the hunger with which he pored over the maps in the back of the promised land.

The illustrated bible had been a bequest to him from his own father whom I remember as very old and very tall, with pale skin – skin I and my father inherited – upright as a ramrod at the age of eighty, dressed like a cleric with a shock of bright white hair. This strange and rarefied man married late in life, raised my father single-handedly after his wife died early, and for the next thirty-five years the two of them lived an extreme and ascetic life at odds with the burgeoning industrial city around them; that is, until my father's thirty-sixth birthday, when he saw my mother at a charity book fair, liked the look of the soft, pallid creature, and began to court her in a manner befitting his honourable nature.

There was another reason for our move, however. I know that my father held towns, or more particularly people, responsible for my mother's periodic lapses into listlessness, sleepiness and weakness, which could last for months on end, leaving her immobilized and us perplexed. It was said to be to do with her heart. In the quiet of the country my father felt sure she would become stronger.

I was a town child, a pale child, a child who read books. Grass growing through concrete, trees with fences around them, a bird-feeder that hung in our backyard and which my father filled religiously, jars of tadpoles on windowsills: these were all the country I knew. I had never smelt wild garlic or heard an owl on winter evenings or seen a badger or a weasel or a stoat. I had never heard a rabbit scream or watched the sun rise over a cornfield, never gone mushroom picking at dawn or found the windpipe of a fox, discarded like a party streamer, in the damp furrows of a field.

I don't remember disliking our town but I do remember

feeling hungry while I lived there, though not for food. After school Elijah our dog and I went to the wasteland where a spiked metal fence separated the houses from the power plant. We played fetch amongst the scrub grass, jumped from discarded girders, ran through plastic piping and climbed concrete blocks from which steel rods protruded like twisted sinews. When it rained Elijah and I sat beneath a flyover that stretched like a monstrous rainbow from one side of the motorway to the other. The concrete was grey, the sky greyer. Drips from the roof made puddles in which petrol flowers bloomed. We went there sometimes when my mother was asleep in bed or when my father was in a black humour. Elijah rested his head on my knee and I cupped my hand around his nose. I think we both dreamt of better times and places.

Despite our excitement at moving, despite the promise it gave, I think we were all a little fearful. Abraham went out from his own country to the place God would show him, he did not ask questions, he did 'just so'. But it is dangerous to set out without knowing where you will arrive. A deer can run only on its own territory; alien land gives it up to its pursuers, which is why deer are carted from place to place and hunted, as men used to be. But if my father was daunted he gave no sign of it. He said: 'God will show us the way.'

Two and a half months before my thirteenth birthday, we drove to the coast and took a ferry. We heard the blare of a horn, unearthly in the darkness, and saw a door like a mouth swing down. We rattled up a ramp into an iron gullet. Inside there were pink walls, seats red as viscera, flickering fluorescent light. The beast smelt of diesel, carpet freshener and the tang of stale vomit.

'I'll be back soon,' I said to Elijah, and stroked his head through the bars of the cage we had to leave him in, in a row of other cages, other dogs. He pressed against the bars, whimpering, his eyes dark, his tail tucked between his legs. It was very hard walking away from him.

We sat below the waterline where there were no windows, thinking this preferable to watching the horizon yo-yo, but both my parents were sick. My father was reduced to an ashen, mild-mannered person I had never encountered before nor since, swaying along the aisle, collapsing watery-legged into his seat. My mother did not move at all, only vomited into a plastic bag on her lap, then tilted her head back.

I wasn't sick. I rode the waves of bile. It was a second-by-second thing, requiring herculean feats of concentration. This is God's plan, I said to myself; we are doing 'just so'; the devil was merely trying to dishearten us by sending winds and high water. Though I had to admit that the substance beyond the ship's walls – which was making it splinter and creak and shudder and groan, which raised it higher than I thought possible, then removed everything beneath it so that it plummeted back into the bowels of the earth and grated sickeningly on what must surely be the sea bottom – did not feel much like water; and, if it was, God was not making a path for us to pass through but setting it in turmoil.

Towards the end even my faith wavered. I had to make a superhuman effort to open my mouth but at one point I asked my mother: 'Are we going to drown?'

My father, unable to move either, said thickly: 'No.'

My mother could not speak at all but she reached out her hand – hot, heavy and damp – and dropped it onto mine. Then she closed her eyes again and the night went on groaning and flickering and grinding. Three hours later we were spewed onto the foreign shore, though whether because of misdemeanour or divine plan I was no longer sure.

*

We came by darkness so we did not see how the dunes gave way to pines, how the pines gave way to gorse, the gorse to fields, and houses appeared. We drove through the night, my mother, my father and I, an eternal trinity – one all-powerful, one all-loving, one all-seeing, not much more than a ghost – while other ghosts trailed white fingers over the bonnet and our faces and the backs of our seats. We arrived at the bungalow we were to rent and the car came to a gravelly stop between pine trees swaying in the night sky, and we smelt real air for the first time, as if we had just been born, reeking of fields and night-time and the wild. We explored rooms fusty with orange and brown carpets, Elijah's tail stiff with excitement – the kitchen with its white Formica and its silky smell of frying fat, the musty, modern hall, the anodyne sitting room and dining room – and we slept shuttered for the first time in complete darkness, with no streetlight, only that of the moon, heads of grass bending this way and that beyond the window, with no sounds but owls in a wood and a mysterious bang every now and then that I later learnt was a crow-scarer.

And when I woke the next morning and stood on the stoep and looked out at the rough grass, the ragged pines, the road shooting past – when I ran up the hill at the back and stood amongst the heads of grass and watched the sun being born – I was born along with it, the past as small as an image reflected in an eye.

I did not know where we had come from; I did not know where we had landed. I would not have known, if someone had asked me, how to get back.

The Covenant

I remember the strangeness of our first weeks on the island but I don't know how to explain it or whether that strangeness accounted for what happened later on. The bungalow was part of it. It had peeling white window frames, a mustard bathroom suite, a gas stove in the kitchen, and in the hall a plastic runner yellow with age. For the months that we lived there, our cupboards and tables and chairs were crowded into the wide sunny front room like miscellanea in a junk shop, and these things reminded us, along with the locked room at the end of the corridor, that the bungalow did not belong to us nor we to it. But we read about Abraham, about how he was obedient, about the covenant God made with him:

'Hear me, Asa and all Judah and Benjamin! The Lord is with you when you are with him, and if you seek him he will let Himself be found by you; but if you abandon him, he will abandon you.' Then Moses came and related to the people all the words of the true God, and all the judicial decisions and all the people answered with one voice and said: 'All the words that the true God has spoken we are willing to do.' So Moses took the blood and sprinkled it upon the people and said: 'Here is the blood of the covenant that the true God has concluded with you as respects all these words.'

'The covenant applies to us too,' my father said. 'If we are obedient we will be blessed. But we have to give God our best.'

I could see the sense of that, but wondered how we

would know God was blessing us. I supposed it would be when my father found work and we found a house.

My father said: 'We were chosen to come here, the need is great.'

But that I was not so sure of – because hadn't we also chosen? Hadn't our need been great?

The island may have been virgin territory as far as *our* god was concerned but others had got there before Him: the bungalow was full of idols. There was an etiolated plaster Virgin, two wooden crucifixes and a picture of a bedraggled and remarkably tranquil Christ, looking heaven-wards, opening his tunic with a delicately curved finger to reveal, in the midst of his deathly-white chest, a bleeding heart ringed with thorns. We discovered the last on the second evening when we turned on the lights in the sitting room. The overhead bulb was dim but in the corner the heart glowed blood red. Coupled with the pathetic, almost coquettish face above, it was both sickly and horrifying. Even my father seemed shocked. Then he laughed, went to the picture, turned it over and pulled out the plug. The heart glowed for a second, then faded; the picture was just a picture again. In relief my mother laughed at herself, but her face was flushed.

There were hundreds of gods in this place, my father said; the island was full of them, gods of the streams and the hills and the trees. We took the bleeding Christ and the other idols to a tin shed that stood at the side of the bungalow beneath the pine trees. He caught my eye as we closed the door on Him and I felt obscurely guilty, as if we were shutting a child in a room and turning out the light.

The first time we went into the town we left Elijah in the kitchen. It was unusual for us to leave him behind and perhaps what happened on that occasion was because we should not have done. It was a breezy day in early April, the country rolling and green and spattered with gorse. There were bungalows along the road, some new houses and one or two old cottages.

'People don't have gardens here, they have fields,' I said. It was true; there were small, mown fields attached to the houses with fences around them, as if there was too much space to be accounted for.

'Plenty of land, you see,' my father said.

Halfway there my father stopped to get petrol and when he went to pay he took the small pocket bible we kept in the glove compartment; we saw him open it while he was talking to the garage attendant. The attendant shook his head slightly and turned away as my father spoke. We saw the affable nod my father gave, his hand raised in farewell. He swung into the car as if he had just found a winning lottery ticket.

'Petrol in!' he said. 'On we go.' Not long after that he began to sing, and we joined him, honking the horn at the chorus.

After another ten minutes the town appeared, shimmering on the far side of an estuary, two steeples pricking sun-clotted clouds. On closer inspection it turned out to be brown and shabby, and with an uncomfortable familiarity like the smell of boiled beef and cabbage in dark passageways. It was a peculiar combination; seafront and wild west, the buildings square, blockish, painted peach, brown, turquoise, dark green, pale blue, purple, burnt orange; the signs on them read McCalls's Medicine Hall, Centenary Stores, Campbell's Trading, Joe's Whisky Bar. I had never seen such ugly buildings nor such odd ones. In the window of a tobacconist's a raffle was advertised; in the newsagent's electrical goods were displayed; at a green-grocer's a cage of chickens squawked just inside the door. Was this what living near the sea did, I wondered: make everything strange and wild and unplaceable?

My father bought a parking ticket from the newsagent's and we parked on the quay. I had never been to a town on a quay, nor seen a railway on one either, and I had certainly never seen all three together. Beneath iron sleepers the sea breathed in and out. Shielding my eyes with my hand I followed the land as far as I could. At the vanishing point, a finger of rock beckoned. It looked like the heel of a shoe, but my father said it was called the Head. I could just about make out a dark forest there.

My father said he was going to get some money from the bank.

'Why don't you start here?' He gestured at the quay and thrust the pocket bible at my mother, who blinked, then said: 'Right.'

She and I stood on the quay. A woman with a bag walked by and my mother said: 'Good morning. Could I share a verse with you from the bible? It has such an inspiring message.'

The woman didn't stop walking, though she did turn her head. My mother looked around. We approached a man with a stick who waved us away with a scowl. 'Go 'way with ya!' he said, and spat on the ground. He seemed to think we were someone else.

My mother laughed. She said: 'Let's try up here.'

We walked towards the boats. Their masts towered into louring clouds that rolled away over the glittering water. We walked to the edge of the quay and my mother held onto my jumper, though I asked her not to. The rusty boats stank, their bellies rising and falling with the lazy swell. The hulls were deep throated and hollow, the boards sodden, teeming with lobster pots, buckets and slime-streaked slabs. On board men were killing eels. Their hands were covered in blood and appeared swollen. I watched the bulging fingers straighten the eels, saw the flash of the knife, the skirmish, then the sudden stillness.

Heads went below, guts to the side. The split eels, suddenly motionless, showed pink as babies' gums. There was a perfection to the movement; one eel replaced another, which was itself split in two, different yet the same; the board cleared, the board bloody; the eel one, the eel two. When the men and the eels didn't change positions at all, the action seemed to replay itself. When they did, when an eel was awkward or the men raised their hands higher, the action seemed infinite.

I felt dazed, my thoughts heavy and slow. I turned to my mother – and that is when I saw the group of children watching from the quayside. They were my own age, twelve perhaps or thirteen, three girls and a boy. One of the girls had pale skin and black hair, and she was watching me, not my mother nor the fishermen. I asked my mother again, in a low voice, not to hold onto my jumper, but she wasn't listening. She hailed one of the fishermen.

'Hello! Could we share a verse with you from the bible?' The man flicked a glance at us but didn't answer. My mother repeated her question. She looked round to see if there was an easier way to communicate and decided there was not. 'Did you know,' she called, 'that Jesus died for you?'

From the corner of my eye I could see the girl with black hair whispering to another. They weren't smiling but there was a light in their faces, an avidity, as if they were pleased with themselves. As if they had found something good.

The fisherman said: 'Sorry, lady.'

My mother called back: 'Couldn't I share this passage with you?' She beamed as she held the bible aloft. One of the men shook his head very slightly. 'Well, have a good day,' she called. They didn't reply.

As we walked away from the boats she was flushed and

still smiling, though the smile was a little fixed. She said: 'Would you like an ice cream?'

I glanced at the children. 'Won't he mind?' I said, meaning my father.

'Oh, don't worry about him,' she said. Her eyes were very bright. It was unlike her.

We passed right by the children and went into a peppermint-green building with darker green squares on the end of it called Sheila's.

My mother seemed happier. She said: 'What do you fancy, my love?' She looked at me. 'Madeline?'

The door had tinkled. A surge of blood passed through me, first hot, then cold. The children had followed us. They were sitting at a table by the door.

I stared hard at the ice creams. 'Vanilla,' I said.

My mother said: 'Don't you want something else?'

'No.'

She looked at me in surprise, as if I had hurt her.

'Thank you,' I said in a low voice.

She said: 'One strawberry and one vanilla, please.'

In the reflection of the ice-cream cabinet I could see the girl with black hair, her gaze fixed on me. Her eyes were blue and her skin was pale. She was pretty, and she was smiling as if I was amusing or a novelty of some kind. My chest felt tight.

My mother handed the cornet to me and I immediately became aware of the way I held it. 'Thank you' suddenly seemed a foolish thing to say. I tried to think of some other word but suddenly all words seemed foolish. My mother was about to sit at a table when I said: 'Let's go outside.'

I crossed the road without waiting for her and stood by the car. I felt sick, as if I had run a long way. When she reached me my mother said: 'Don't ever cross the road without waiting for me again.'

'I'm sorry,' I said. I still could not bring myself to begin the ice cream.

'What's the matter?' she said.

'Nothing,' I said.

We got back into the car. I turned and looked out of the window. The children had come out of the shop. They didn't have ice creams. They had gone in just to watch me, as if I was some weird animal. When they looked around for me, I ducked down in the back seat. I wished Elijah was there. No one ever laughed at him.

I listened to my mother eat her ice cream. Then she turned around and said: 'Give it to me,' and I handed her mine.

We heard a shout and there was my father striding along the quay. His jacket was slung over his shoulder and he was whistling loudly. I saw the children become still when they saw him. He swung himself into the front seat and said: 'Ice creams.'

My mother nodded.

'No money,' he said. 'The bank's on strike.'

My mother stopped eating. 'On strike?'

'Aye, we'll have to make do with the cash we brought over.' His eyes were shining. He didn't seem to think it was bad news at all.

My mother looked straight ahead. She said: 'Did you see any work advertised?'

'No.'

She turned to him.

'It'll work out, don't worry. Did you have any good discussions?'

'No,' my mother said, in a deeper voice, flatter, weary, with no hint of pretence. She would usually have lied to him.

'Well, you tried, that's the main thing,' he said. With his hand along the back of her seat, he began to reverse.

The children's eyes followed me as we pulled out. I lowered my head and studied the pattern of the stitching on the back of my father's seat, the way one stitch replaced the next, the way the staples held the leather tight. Then the endlessness of it was suddenly too great and I could not look any more.

That afternoon we shopped at a supermarket that we reached through a covered walkway between an electrical and a sports shop. The supermarket was like a warehouse with high white ceilings and crates of unpacked boxes. A song was playing over and over. It went: 'Better by day, better by night, better buy here to get it right!' The words were like a chain that kept revolving. They made me think of the stitches, and then I thought of the men killing eels, and if I managed to push one image out of my mind, the others took its place.

My mother bought fruit and vegetables. I noticed that not many of the other people did, that most of the other people looked as if they had just been gardening or come off a farm. The other women weren't wearing make-up as my mother was, their hair wasn't blow-dried, and they were wearing jeans and fleeces and T-shirts. I could see one woman's nipples. At the checkout my mother looked closely at the new coins and the cashier had to find the right change for her. The cashier had rosy cheeks and was as broad as a man. Her hair was brown and wiry and parted at the side like someone from an old film. My mother thanked her warmly but she didn't smile back and rammed the till closed. I took two bags of shopping from my mother, though she protested, and held onto her hand. I wanted to tell her about the children once we were back at the bungalow but I knew that I wouldn't. She would try to think of something to say and she would worry.

On the way home my father whistled but did not honk the horn. I couldn't sing along now and neither could my mother. I glanced at her face in the mirror. It looked as if the props had been removed from it. I tried to read her eyes but they were glazed and empty.

For the next few days my mother and I made a tunnel through the gorse that grew on the bank at the back of the bungalow. We worked for hours, our arms covered in scratches, slashing at the branches that snapped with tiny puffs of dust. On the third day we broke through to the other side where there was a quarry with stony banks, a lake of cobalt water at the bottom. I was glad to be with my mother because then I could watch her. Thwacking away at the gorse, she seemed to be happy, to have forgotten the town, the fact that my father did not have a job and the bank strike. But over the coming weeks she stayed indoors more and more, and I went to the quarry mostly with Elijah, who sat panting, blinking at the sun, while I dug myself into the shale, a peculiar weight in my chest, and let the sun's light wipe me out. I replayed what had happened in the town. I turned it around in my head and looked for the hidden truth but it was like the water at the bottom of the quarry, which glittered, drew you in, but revealed nothing beneath the surface.

Time spent at the bungalow now felt like a reprieve. I felt sick whenever we went into town. I saw that I was wrong to think life would be bright and balmy on the island, full of the feeling of school holidays and weekends. In some ways it was worse than being in school. Father and Mother had thought I would be better off not mixing any longer with unbelievers. But with my being removed from people completely, I found any contact doubly intense. School had given me a skin of sorts, albeit a painful one. Now I had no skin, or I was shedding the one that I had. We all seemed to be shedding something.

My mother was glowing but restless. She cleaned out cupboards, beat carpets, made a timetable for schoolwork that we never got round to, sewed a new cover for our three-piece suite and painted the wicker furniture on the stoep, forgetting to cover the steps; then had a frantic few hours washing paint off before my father came back.

My father was leaner than I had ever seen him; his hair bristled with purpose, his eyes gleaming. I could smell his skin and his hair when he came in from sawing a fallen pine or from mowing the wild grass at the front of the bungalow with an old mower that tore the grass rather than cut it; I remember the vehemence with which he pushed it, almost tripping as the wheels shot forward. I saw him one day on the stoep with a look on his face that was feral, and when he caught my eye he shifted as if I had disturbed him and said, almost savagely: 'All right?' He was wearing a pair of bright blue shorts.

'Yes,' I said; I was going to say: 'Are you?' but thought better of it.

He set off around the side of the bungalow, the sinews in his legs taut and athletic, covered in virile blond fuzz.

Every day he went into town to see whether the bank was open, if he could find a house or find work. It wasn't, he couldn't, and there was none, but everything was 'wonderful', the roads not riddled with potholes but full of 'character'; people weren't rude but 'gave it to you straight'; the water was the best thing he had ever tasted; the young people were respectful – two said 'Good evening' to him in town (I thought it might have been sarcastic; something to do with the fact that he was wearing a tweed suit and twirling a stick). To my father the island was still a paradise, and we were as good as on holiday.

It was true that those first two months at the bungalow had the loosely woven feel of a holiday, but it was a disconcerting one: time was dislocated and the story unravelling. Sometimes, when we could make ourselves, my mother and I did schoolwork. It was strange working for her. I wanted to try harder but often I tried less. Perhaps she had the same problem, because as often as we studied Pythagoras, we studied buttercups, as often made pies as pie-charts, as often wrote songs on a guitar with four strings as wrote essays – all while Elijah waited in the open door with his head on his paws, his ears pricking at the merest suggestion that class was over.

Sometimes we went walking. There were things to be learnt outdoors too, my mother said. The lanes were breezy, the mornings long, the skies benign, the clouds rolling. It felt peculiar to be wearing dungarees at eleven in the morning.

'Will I ever go back to school?' I said. I meant: go back to life.

'I shouldn't think so.'

'What will I do when I'm grown up?'

'There are lots of things you could do,' she said.

I couldn't think of a single one.

That spring was crisper than any I had known. There were new flowers in dark soil and freshness in the mornings that stirred my stomach. At dusk you could see for miles through bare branches across fields laden with emptiness. There was pink in the sky near the earth. It looked raw, it looked cold, and there was a quiet that spoke of great distances. The land, like us, seemed to be expectant. I would walk back to the bungalow in the evening, and the light would be pink and golden, and the fields already asleep. The distant sounds of cows, the purr of a tractor, the retreating rush of a car or a van on the road made the world seem endlessly spacious and endlessly light. Every so often the treetops surged as if stroked by some invisible hand, the fields kept on rolling and surging; they jostled and shimmered and gave way to each other, hill after hill, rising and falling like swells in the sea, and in the endlessness of it all – in the grasses, in the dizzy activity of butterflies and birds – a chink sometimes opened, and on the brightest of days the world grew suddenly darker and suddenly still.

I had always wanted to know God, to be close to Him, feel His presence beyond doubt, to be 'One' with Him, if that was possible. What else was a child raised to think of God constantly expected to do? It was as natural to want God to pay attention to me as it would have been to want to be acknowledged by an absent parent. It was as natural to want to feel some sort of union with Him as it was to desire union with an absent lover. Of course, if other things are missing, that desire may be stronger.

When I look back now, I don't really know what my essential motivations were, but I remember it wasn't long after we arrived on the island that I promised I would find God. Such a discovery would be an absolution, I reasoned; an absolution, and an absorption into something larger. I had realized, lying in the shale with the weight in my chest, that this was what I wanted. Did not God dissolve even as He protected and excise even as He embraced?

I heard that men had seen God in fields, glimpsed His face in rivers and clouds. Jesus taught in the countryside, watched suns rise, passed through vineyards and olive groves, fields of barley and wheat; if I was to find God what better place than the country to look? What was more, I thought I was on the right track.

'I think I've discovered something,' I said to my mother when we were walking one morning.

'What?'

'Lots of small particles, buzzing like snow.'

'Where?' she said.

'Everywhere.' I pointed to the hedgerow, I pointed to the air.

She looked. 'I can't see anything.'

'It's like atoms,' I said.

'You can't see atoms.'

I said: 'It's particles of God. I see them in the evening too in the barley field, and in the morning when the sun hits the water in the quarry.'

My mother said: 'Perhaps you need glasses.'

'No,' I said. 'They're real.'

We carried on walking. She looked worried. To distract her I trod on her shoes, then she trod on mine, then I ran off and she raced me. We drew neck-and-neck and I caught her around the middle and swept her nearly off her feet while Elijah jumped around us, barking.

Many days we spent in balmy lanes with bibles and bags. We rarely got to open the bags, much less the bibles, and sometimes people's doors shut before we had begun speaking. I don't know how they knew who we were. My father strode ahead of us, whistling loudly. Although on maps the island was small, from the inside it seemed to be vast. Lanes led onto others, roads stretched in straight lines for miles. My father walked on, filling his lungs, calling: 'Look at that!' We followed in long skirts that clung to tights that furrowed at ankles, blouses buttoned to the neck and cardigans buttoned over blouses. Breezes lifted the hairs on my arms, my nipples grazed cotton, my collar chafed, seams scratched, labels made me itch, fabric twisted, creased and clung; my shoes rubbed. Before, I had never noticed my skin, nor my clothes, but suddenly the two seemed incompatible. When we got home I tore my clothes off and threw on a holey jumper and dungarees. Sometimes I went out barefoot with a stick.

I kept watch for the particles. It was on the mornings when my mother and I were walking that I saw them most. We'd go for miles, I in a sort of trance, and there they were, eddying, jostling one another, floating around me. They were a little like the dots in the paintings by the Dutch man in a book of my mother's. Those paintings were filled with just such dabs: blue, turquoise, magenta, green. I didn't mention them to my mother again for fear of worrying her, but I thought about them. Were they the stuff everything was made of, I wondered, that was always in motion? I was sure that if I looked long enough and thought hard enough, I would be able to learn something.

I was noticing other things too, too many to keep count of. The air, for example, was like no air I had ever encountered: it pricked and pierced, even on warm days. The light seemed to be wilder, to come from a different place than any light I had seen before; it also seemed to me to be terribly bright. These things were not unusual enough to talk about, but they were different enough to let me know I had better pay attention. The whole island was a book I couldn't decipher and it evoked feelings I had no sphere of reference for. I could not say I was happy or sad or excited or afraid. Those words were all inadequate. That is why I began writing the journal in the beginning, and why from that time onwards I always carried it with me, in an attempt to turn the nebulous into something I could read, or at least put down in words:

A man in a suit walking along the road with a briefcase in his hand and a rucksack on his back covered with polythene . . .

A man in a shop who growled at his son like a dog . . .

Thirty-five geese that flew by . . .

A dead cat with white eyes on the road . . .

A man firing a gun, rooks everywhere . . .

A woman screaming: 'Don't look at them!' Holding cross up . . .

No gardens but small, mown fields with fences . . .

Processions of cars following hearses . . .

Sunday, people dressing up and going to the three big churches in town . . .

The smell of dead animals on the side of the road. Brown, beige, sickly. Pink. Purple. Little flies.

Throughout that spring we continued to preach. It was our offering, the fruit of lips, my father said. Christ died for the world, could save lives if his sacrifice were known, and it was our responsibility to tell people about it. Mornings were times of porridge and prayer. Porridge was cheap, prayer was invaluable. We sat at the Formica table by the kitchen window while the sun rose over the barley field. My father said: 'Thank you for this day, bless our efforts, forgive us our sins.' The prayer having been said, spoons descended on the glutinous mess, slow farts pocking obscenely, then shrinking back into spermatic soup. The remainder settled into a tepid brown tarpaulin scaly to the tap of a spoon. At the table we read about Moses getting up early in the morning and building an altar at the foot of the mountain. We read about God producing the manna and sending the quail and making the rock spout. 'Bless us, forgive us, give us this day—' but my father did not find work and the bank did not open and the shops would not cash his cheques.

Towards the end of April my mother began making bread (it was cheaper than buying it), rolling the elastic dough, furling it under and flinging it up with a floury bang. It smelt cold and fleshy, her offering, uncomfortably human; it had to sleep for a night before it could function and when we weren't looking it grew magically beneath a tea towel. Then she murdered it all over again and shut it in the oven, where it rose, splitting and golden, smelling of savouriness.

My father made more enquiries about work, more trips

to the bank, more prayerful petitions. He shook the gas bottle hard and made a reserve can of petrol. The banks would open soon, he said. My mother said of course they would and smiled at me. The tadpoles I caught in the quarry began clinging to the lid of their bucket, their eyes black with the implacable fury of frogs. Elijah caught rabbits and my mother skinned and roasted them or put them in stews.

'We can't afford not to,' she said.

'You get used to that in the country,' my father said. 'You see where things really come from.'

I refused to eat the rabbits, but I couldn't avoid knowing how good they tasted because the gravy was flavoured with them and the kitchen filled with their aroma.

The field at the back of the bungalow broke out into gold, honeysuckle tapped at the sitting room window, a cuckoo could be heard in the thicket. We went out in the car less and less and when we did my father switched the engine off to go downhill. We had 'reserve' petrol in one can and 'reserve, reserve' in another. We had to buy groceries in the garage because the supermarket would not cash my father's cheques. It was twice as expensive as the supermarket but he didn't complain.

'God will provide,' he said.

Towards the end of our time at the bungalow we began to notice one another, we coughed for no reason in each other's company; awkward, as if we were strangers; we jiggled our feet. We were playing house, staying up past our bedtime, camping out on our own. We were watched, or behaved as if we were. One evening of warm rain when the light wouldn't go we played catch. We became conscious of our bodies in the strange light. My father took charge – 'Left a bit! Further back!' He tore about, the high-school athlete; my mother was blotchy, panting, tormented by gnats. I jumped and ran faster than necessary.

The game went on too long, our smiles became tight, our shouts half-hearted, the land closer, the stillness disturbing. We were children putting on a play, but there was no audience except rabbits and bats. It darkened at last. There was no one to call us in but we went anyway, proclaiming our fun, aware that something, somewhere, was not right.

Sediment

Dr Lucas says it is not uncommon for there to be a crossover between the conscious and the unconscious during hypnotic retrieval, that the past can be thought of as a layer of sediment at the bottom of a pool, which when stirred rises in flurries. This often results, he said, in loss of clarity for a while.

Since my therapy began, things from long ago, sounds, smells and textures, have been flooding back. I look up from a book, I wake at night, the sky takes on a particular hue, there is a velocity in the air – and I am back at the farm, something gives way and suddenly beneath my fingers are not words but a gatepost, not paper but the bark of a pine. Just now I was woken by someone running by with a trolley and I was back in the courtyard the night we chased the horses with saucepans. I heard the sound of hooves on cobblestones, saw the whites of their eyes, the steam from their nostrils. I could smell the stench of oil and grass, of manure and water. At such times I wonder whether lives interrupted run on parallel lines, whether there are times that stretch out and have a life of their own, continuing somewhere else in the ether, and during those times what is impossible becomes possible and what is unreal, real.

In the Platnauer Room I travel back with the doctor. Twice now, as I have gone under, I have had the impression I was standing on the bank of a river. A field of white flowers lies behind me. The low light is blinding the fields as it dies. I wade into the water. When it reaches my jaw I slip under. For a moment there are ripples, then all trace of me vanishes. When I return to the surface it is either calmly – forehead, nose, neck, breasts – or all at once, gasping and shedding droplets. The doctor is the redeemer. He brings me back. Time and again, no matter what has happened in that nether region, the Platnauer Room appears in all its warm insincerity. Time and again, I stand once more on the bank of myself, shiver and rub myself dry.

'We're making excellent progress,' Dr Lucas says. He looks jubilant, his eyes glittering more than ever. 'You're highly hypnotizable, Madeline, as is often the case with amnesia sufferers.'

I sit on the couch, reorientating myself. The Platnauer Room basks in the glow of feigned intimacy conferred by the table lamps and soft furnishings. I was glad to see when I came in today that the irises had finally been replaced by arum lilies. So far they are having no effect on me at all.

He scribbles in the notepad. 'How are you feeling?'

'Tired.'

A white face peers back at me in the window, reflected in the glow. It looks frozen, like an insect caught in amber or a foetus in formaldehyde. I turn back to the room.

'So what have you discovered?' I say, sceptical and at the same time curious to know.

'That the farm was much more than a place to you; it's the site of a personal mythology.'

In spite of myself I am rather impressed by the sound of this. But I laugh and say: 'You mean I've made the whole thing up?'

'No,' he says, 'though really it sometimes matters less what a patient fabricates than the reasons they may have for doing so; but no, in this case what I am saying is – well, you know what a myth is, don't you?'

'A story,' I say.

'Yes; an account, passed down through generations, usually of a key event in the history of a people or some sort of phenomenon – often involving a supernatural being. The year at the farm made such an impression upon you that you have effectively explained yourself by means of it; your reason for living is there; and your reason for dying. Your story began and ended within that small radius. We're out of the story altogether at the moment, we're languishing in an appendix, we're stuck in a footnote – perhaps we're not even in the book proper at all, but on the flyleaf, in the small print. You can't begin a new book because you can't close this one. Someone has whitened the words out – *you* whitened them out but you've forgotten. We've got to retrace them, and you have to find the courage to read them out, for the first time, to me. And when we have both heard them the book can be closed and reshelved, and you can begin reading something else.'

There is an uncomfortable sensation in my sternum. I swallow but it doesn't disappear.

'D'you see?'

'Yes.'

'How long were you at the bungalow before you found the farm, Madeline?'

'Two months.'

'Did your father manage to find work before you moved?'

'No. But by that time the bank strike had ended.'

'You seem to have been troubled by money constantly.'

'We trusted it would work out.'

'Because God would provide for you.'

'Yes.'

'And He stopped helping you because—'

I flush. 'I told you.'

'Remind me again.'

'Because of sin.'

'You sinned?'

My heart beats hard. 'They did – she did – I did; what does it matter?'

He inhales, as if deciding something, and says: 'I'd like to go forward to the day you discovered the farm, the very first glimpse of it. Can you tell me about that?'

The Farm

It is May, early afternoon. My father comes into the kitchen long enough to say: 'There's a farm for sale.' By the time my mother puts down the tea towel he has gone. He is waiting in the car when we get outside and begins to drive before she has shut the door.

We went through town and followed the river. Where the land flattened we turned left at a bridge into a tunnel of trees; shade closed over us like a hand and a bird clattered away, calling. The hedges were filled with wild garlic. Branches brushed at my hair. We came out of the trees and the road rose in front of us. The sun was lustrous, roughened at the edges like silk. We were afloat that afternoon, setting sail, and reflected upside down in the bonnet of the car, sky, trees and clouds were also sailing. At the top of a hill where a line of three trees stood like sentinels against the sky we turned left. A rutted track led upwards and I caught the smell of bindweed and thyme. The higher we climbed, the stranger I felt. Was it then I remembered it?

The track wound steeply between wrestling hedges. Fields fell away on either side into the blue. At the top a gate, paint flaking, swung wide under my hand and we drove into a courtyard blanched by heat. The barns were red roofed, whitewashed, crumbling; the house damp, dark: a dark house standing in its own shadow, beneath towering clouds.

*

We got out and shut the car doors and the noise they made was instantly swallowed as if it had never existed. The only sound was the rushing of a slight breeze and a faraway tinkling that summer days seem to contain. My father's eyes became soft, almost sad, I thought. He stood there just looking.

There was a whitewashed dairy and sheds and a stone kennel by the gate with a sloping red roof. The courtyard was large, the house white, except where damp seeped from its edges. It had been quite grand once, you could see; there were elaborate gate pillars and a porch. A water-pump with a very tall handle stood in the middle of the courtyard, a wall capped with a hedge separated the garden from the house, and through an archway I could see a tall pine covered in creeper, the shape of its uppermost part suggesting a giant question mark.

This was the place, the season late May. We stayed all afternoon.

I don't know if it was because I was very hot or very excited, or because I was still feeling as if I had seen the place before, but it occurred to me that every surface in this place had been written upon. Perhaps the thought simply presented itself because there were layers upon layers: whitewash, paint, damp, rust, creepers, moss. The 'words' were unreadable, scribbled over and under one another, not in lines but in clusters, as cells might burgeon, or marginalia; as if once upon a time some attentive reader had seen fit to annotate this place to an obsessive degree, one asterisk leading to another, and another, a footnote referencing itself. I traced the text with my eyes, along the bottoms of the walls, along the guttering and eaves, in between cobbles, across the corrugated roofs of the sheds and the fine grass threading from the middle of the courtyard to the bottom of the drive, like body hair descending from a navel.

There were more puzzles: the cobbles in the courtyard spelt out three numbers: two, four, and eight, and we could not see why until my father suggested that the water-pump was a sundial. At the end of the house in the courtyard there were steps set into a waist-high wall enclosing a semicircular pit. Railings ran along the top of it and a gate was set into the wall and a tap into one side, and there was a hole in the ground like a plug. My mother speculated that it was an ancient sheep-dip. There was a machine in the dairy that was taller than me and filled the whole room, with wooden paddles and wheels that no one knew what to make of. The barn was the most impenetrable place of all because it was so dark. Where the light did shine through, in chinks and nooks and a tiny smeared window, weeds grew and spiders spun, but the rest was a medley of gleams, streaks, blotches and objects that loomed half formed out of shadows.

Beside the front door of the house, as if in some sort of welcome, stood a thick stone wheel that glinted, with a hole bored into its centre, from which ran a long red line. I thought it was some sort of altar and the suspicion was confirmed when I touched the line and smelt my finger. It smelt like iron.

'A millstone,' my father said.

'What's this?' I said, pointing to the red.

'Rust. Where the spoke went through.'

'Oh,' I said.

My father struggled with the front door, then it budged suddenly and with an odorous gush of damp we found ourselves in the hall. Inside the house the inscriptions continued: ivy had made its way in at the top of the door and bindweed at the bottom. A trail of ants was marching across the tiles; the door frames were full of tiny round holes; mould had made delicate patterns on the walls; and something had left a stain where the light could not reach it, a strange shape, like a star. To the right, in the linoleum-floored kitchen, damp made the walls bubble and bulge, and the hot sills were mottled with spider dung.

In an alcove at the side of a woodstove was a statue of the Virgin.

'That'll have to go,' my father said.

So he had decided already; the house would be ours. He strode around those rooms as if someone were timing him; he had seen all he needed to see of the kitchen and utility room while my mother and I were still exploring the hall. We heard him shout: 'Look at this!' and arrived in the doorway of a large room in time to see him stagger backwards from the window in a shower of wood flakes. His face was rapturous.

'They've got the old shutters!' he said. He tried to put back the shutter but had to settle for propping it against the wall. 'Nothing that a few screws won't fix!'

My mother stood at the window, looking into the garden. She was rosy-cheeked, as though she had just woken to a wonderful surprise.

'Can you imagine yourself here?' my father said.

'Yes,' she said. She inhaled deeply and then let her breath go, giving him a look intended only for the two of them.

Beside the fireplace there were wall cupboards and, inside, many old books.

'Ready-made library!' my father said to me. I think he expected that to sell the place to me.

We went back into the kitchen. In one corner, stairs led upwards. I went last, trailing my hand over the banister that had been painted so many times it was both sticky and slippery. A corridor ran along the back of the house and we went into each of the bedrooms leading off it, Elijah's claws clattering on the floor, his tail swinging this way and that like a flag moving ahead of troops.

My father bent down to look out of the windows, saying: 'Look at that view!'

Festoons of wrinkled paper hung from the walls. The wood beneath our feet, the door frames and the window frames were rotten. He didn't seem to notice. Nor did my mother, who whispered: 'They've got the old floorboards!'

The door at the end of the landing was closed but I could see light streaming out through the chinks around it. I lifted the latch and knew as I stepped inside that if the house became ours this room would be mine. From the windows I could see the country all around, right to some blue mountains. The window creaked as I opened it, a graduated creak, like the chug of a tiny engine. Elijah jumped up and put his front paws on the sill so that they rested beside my elbows, and I put my arm around him and hugged him tight.

When we went outside again the sun was a weight on our heads and shoulders. Elijah bounded through the gate beneath the arch covered with ivy and we followed. The trees crowded around, each vista giving onto another, and I felt peculiar again, not myself, as if I had been here before. It was then I remembered; I turned and there was the tall tree – a pine this time – no angels nor sword. I don't know why I did not tell them then about the picture in the front of the big bible, but for the first time the island did not seem new to me but old: old land we had known a long time ago that had just been restored to us.

We explored, the grass up to our waists, the ground hummocky underfoot. It was like walking in a graveyard, and again I thought of those dead gods. There was an orchard, the remains of a herb garden and box hedges.

My mother said: 'Look at the trees!'

My father said: 'Look at the view!'

There were flowers I did not know all the names of then: lupins, pinks, red-hot pokers, rhododendrons, broom and, beneath the apple trees, odd, flesh-coloured orchids that smelt putrid.

'Look at this!' I heard my father cry. He was standing below a wild bees' nest. 'The land of milk and honey!' he said, grabbed my mother by the hand and swung her around in an arc. She gave a cry, ungainly with embarrassment and delight, and Elijah bounced around them, barking. 'I think we've found it,' he said to her. She nodded. They joined hands and walked back to the house.

But Elijah and I ran to the bottom of the garden through the grass, me lifting my knees high like a pony, he bouncing as if there were springs in his paws, and when we came to a bank of brambles, wild roses, strawberries, elderflower, a birch wood and a stream, I pushed through a gap next to a sign that read: 'Trespassers Will Be Prosecuted'. I was unsure whether it pointed within or without. Elijah scrambled through after me and we stood panting in the long meadow beyond: cows staring with rheumy eyes through thick lashes, my pulse beating low in my body. There was a river at the bottom of the field.

On the way back up through the garden I stood at the foot of the tall pine, gazing up through the ivy. I was trying to see how things would go here. I wanted some sort of indicator. I remembered the woman in the picture in the front of the large bible, the woman with the white face; the creeper that coiled in a poisonous embrace around her wrist; the other that shackled her partner's ankle. I remembered the dog howling silently and the chimpanzee covering its mouth as if at some unutterable horror. But the creepers around this tree were warm, dry and still, and the tree smelt good. Elijah looked at me happily, his tongue rippling in his open mouth, his eyes wild. I left the tree and trailed him back to the house.

My parents were having tea from a flask in the herb garden, leaning their backs against the end wall of the house surrounded by the box hedges. It was then that we heard a voice from the courtyard.

'Where are y' hiding?' it bellowed.

Elijah began to bark and tore through the ivy-covered gateway. We followed. A man was standing on the stroke of three in the courtyard. String held his coat around his waist, corduroy trousers with baggy knees ended too far above his socks, and the soles on his trainers were coming away. His cheeks were windburnt but his eyes were very pale, as if they had been blanched by the sun and rain. Elijah was barking incessantly. I told him to stop, to come to me.

Then I ran to Elijah but he skirted me, his hackles high, still barking. I tried to catch hold of his collar and couldn't, and it was only when my father yelled at him that he turned reluctantly and slunk to my side.

The man grinned, his eyes wide and vacant. 'Good little guard dog, isn't he?' he cackled. 'You might need him here!' He coughed after he laughed and couldn't stop, then spat on the cobbles.

'Who are you?' my father said.

'Who are *you*?' the man replied, and his milky gaze passed over all three of us.

'We're just looking around,' my father said, after a moment.

'Ah, you're the new folk moving in,' said the fellow. 'He'll not like it, I can tell you. He won't like it a bit!'

'What are you talking about?' my father said.

'Him who was here before!'

I caught a whiff of urine on the afternoon breeze, sweet, acrid, animal.

'The place hasn't been occupied for years,' my father said.

'That's right,' said the man. 'But *he's* still here; *he'll* never leave!'

Elijah began to bark again. My father raised his hand to him and he ducked and went quiet.

The man grinned, revealing yellow, pointed teeth. 'Are ye going to buy it then?'

My father said firmly: 'We're just looking.'

'It's not been lived in since they took him away – I was there when it happened!' The pale eyes slid towards my mother, who looked frightened.

My father said: 'I think it'd be better if you went.'

The man laughed. 'Aye, I'll go – but he'll not!' He shambled away. 'Ye'll see!' he called. 'Good luck! Good luck to ye!'

Elijah twisted away from me and began barking again. The stranger waved. He waved again as he went through the gate, and once more as he disappeared around the corner of the drive. We did not seem to be able to move from the spot.

'Who was that?' my mother said. She was laughing half-heartedly but her eyes were frightened.

My father was glowering at us as if it was our fault. 'Some local nutcase, by the looks of it. Off his head. Oh, you get them around these parts, you get them all right!'

We went back to the garden but it was different and we left shortly after. First the house, then the barns were hidden in the curve of the track and then the track too was lost in the lane.

My parents forgot about the stranger as they neared the town and began to talk about the farm again, about how perfect it was.

We parked on the quay and they went shopping. The shops still would not cash my father's cheques and we had to buy groceries in the garage on the way home but that day my father didn't complain.

On the straight stretch near the bungalow he took his

hands off the steering wheel and when my mother cried out and grabbed it, he pulled her towards him and kissed her head.

'I'll make an offer first thing tomorrow,' my father said.

At dinner he thanked God, not for helping us find a house but for bringing us home.

The Tree and the Root

All right: so I am an inmate in an asylum for the mentally insane, but what is sanity anyway? Galileo they imprisoned, Socrates they poisoned, Jesus they crucified. 'The Word was in the world, and . . . the world knew him not. He came unto his own, but his own received him not.' Paul says that God chose the foolish things of the world to confound the wise, and the weak to confound the mighty. And I know Lucas is the doctor here, and I am the lunatic, but I believe his treatment programme is crazy. Even Margaret has doubts.

'I've never seen anything like it,' she said.

Each day this week I have tried to walk for half a minute longer, I have tried to do three more stretches, I have graded each exercise and challenged each negative thought, and noted whether I succeeded; I have not. Getting up is now by far the worst part of the day. The exhaustion and nausea render me so useless that by the second round of stretches I have to go back to bed.

'Three more,' Margaret says.

She is holding my feet while I raise my arms above my head. Then, arms outstretched, I try to sit up. I try to focus on other things – anything: it is misty; though it has gone nine, it is as dark as evening outside the high window, which makes the fluorescent light even more nightmarish; I can hear the breakfast trolley rattling down the corridor and the door of the dining room open and close; Robyn is wailing; she has not been allowed any more jam. It is no use. I lie back and close my eyes.

'Two more,' Margaret says.

I clench my teeth and stretch my arms out again, the muscles juddering, but this time the nausea is so strong I retch and double up. Determined as I am not to let Lucas win, it is no use. My muscles feel as though they have been soaked in acid, my whole body is awash with heat. I feel a surge of rage at its uselessness and turn my face away so Margaret won't see me cry.

She says: 'Let's get you into bed.' Then she goes to the graph on the wall; I don't know what she writes there. This is how it begins. My body and I are divided and never the twain shall meet.

I believe that my illness is nothing more than an expression of disgust. This disgust is twofold: disgust at the place in which I find myself, and disgust at myself for being here. I am toxic, loaded with residue that must continually surface. The symptoms are messages of some kind but doctors cannot read them. They mark me down as a lost cause. I make no sense, a non-signifier, a non sequitur. I too once looked for patterns, messages, signs, before giving up and learning to live with the mystery. All ailments bespeak corruption at some level. If the tree bears rotten fruit, badness won't be far from the roots. The corruption may be conscious or unconscious but it is there all the same. Sin lives on in bones and blood; what is reaped is what is sowed. On the farm there was an apple tree that smelt like rotting flesh though no defect was outwardly visible. Only when the trunk snapped in a high wind did we see that inside it was red and gory, teeming with glistening nodules soft enough to squeeze between finger and thumb. The smell of it burning filled the house and the garden for days.

I inspect my body daily, but it is only for a few days each month I can expunge all trace of decay. Only then do I have the means to inflict punishment unnoticed. First there is pleasure, then there is pain. Laxatives, sharp implements and disinfectants are kept out of my reach but I manage to purify myself in my own way. A dry flannel can scour, paper can cut, radiators can burn, salt can strip. Blood is the most important thing; there must be blood. And I have a way to manage it without detection, the wounds I inflict lost in the larger wound of womankind. I plan meticulously, I take precautions. Clean instruments are a must. All absolution takes is ingenuity, determination and a little patience.

It is now just after six and I am curled on the bed, moving my foot back and forth. After Margaret left I slept. When I woke I felt anxious so I did the breathing as Lucas instructed: in – two, three, four, five, six; out – two, three, four, five, six. I visualized floating in a warm place. I did stretches every five minutes, varying my position from left side to right, from right side to stomach, from stomach to back, from back to recovery position, and from recovery position to back again.

I described the situation (alone in room), noted initial thoughts about situation (want to get out), wrote down feelings as a result of initial thoughts (fear), challenges to initial thoughts (I am progressing), feelings after challenges (fear), reassessed the situation (alone in room; fear), second thoughts about the situation (see reassessment of situation), feelings as a result of new thoughts (see second thoughts about situation) and completed a second reassessment (alone in room, *substantial* fear). I wrote in the 'What I Did Next' box: 'Filled in another CBT form', and noted that I felt approximately thirty-five per cent more anxious than before. That was when I asked to take a shower.

'How you feeling?'

My heart skips but I don't think my voice betrays me. 'A bit better, thank you, Margaret.'

She sits on the edge of the bed. 'Do you feel well enough to come and have some tea?'

'No,' I say, smiling quickly. 'Not today . . .'

She sees me hold my stomach as I turn, though in fact the pain is in a different place. 'D'you need some pain-killers?' she says.

I am trying to concentrate on what she is saying but it is difficult because I have had to stop moving my foot, which is in itself painful at this particular moment.

'It'll be fine – I'm fine,' I say.

She goes out and I curl back on my side. I am throbbing so much that something seems to be radiating from within. A droplet of sweat slips down my back. I feel better than I have done in days, but even now, when I have managed to purge myself, the situation is not ideal. All I have done is attend to the branches. I cannot reach the root. That is impossible and would require complete disassembly.

The Gift

I go along to the Platnauer Room today ready to be co-operative. I have taken painkillers. There is no reason why things should not go smoothly. It's lighter this evening, winter is drawing to a close. Tonight, however, that fact only makes my stomach churn a little more.

He is in his black leather seat, pencil ready. He is always writing, this doctor, a diligent scribe.

'You moved into the farm not long after you first saw it?'

'That's right.'

'Did your father buy it outright?'

'Yes, he got it cheaply at an auction in a hotel in the town.'

'Did you find out what the vagrant was talking about?'

'Apparently the previous owner had hanged himself from one of the trees in the garden.'

'And this made no difference to your parents?'

'They were too in love with the farm to care.'

'Were there many bidders at the auction?'

'I think my father said the only other bidder was a farmer whose face was hidden beneath his cap.'

'Can you remember moving in?'

Yes, I remember. The sun was higher that day, the air not yet cooling. We made trips in a van. Going up the track, the exhaust came off and it filled with grass and earth, and we went back through the town, sounding like a racing car. My father told us to keep a lookout for police. It was evening before we finished unloading. We took the Virgin outside and smashed her against the wall. She stayed on the cobbles that night, her porcelain flesh in hundreds of pieces.

'We don't need idols,' my father said. 'We've got the real thing.'

I tell the doctor this, but nothing I say will explain what the first day was really like; the strangeness of running through the grass to the bottom of the garden with Elijah, knowing the earth beneath us was our own; the oddness of our teapot and dresser and toothbrushes in those rooms; my father's bird-feeder hanging from one of the apple trees in the garden, not from a nail in a yard; the heap of furniture we left that first night in the courtyard; or the meal we ate beneath the apple trees, using whatever cutlery and plates we could find, my father ravenous, his face red; the way he said: 'We could open the garden to visitors – we could let the dairy and the outbuildings as holiday cottages!'; the way my mother said: 'We could have a tearoom in the barn and serve afternoon teas!' and he did not contradict her; my mother's face glowing like a child's; how she bent her head and made her movements small to fit his; a thing she did when she was happy, with something affected about it.

We stayed up late unpacking, the cool darkness lapping at our legs and arms. Every so often one of us would call from various parts of the garden or house: 'Look at this—' and the other two would come to look, or shout back: 'What?' and we would reply: 'A secret cupboard!' 'The size of this attic!' 'This little thing in the wall—' The house didn't seem to mind the disturbance, its windows open to the fading light; its floors creaked with faux-serious groans, as if it were a sleeper half happy to be woken.

I spent a long time cleaning out the stone kennel by the gate. I swept the floor of old hay, and then the walls and ceiling, which showered me in cobwebs and flakes of white-wash. I scrubbed the shed and propped the door open with a stone to dry.

'Now we just have to find you some fresh straw,' I said to Elijah, and in the hayloft over the wall I found some. 'Look,' I said. 'Look how comfy this is,' making a hollow for him, but he stood in the doorway of the kennel with his tail between his legs. 'You've never had a kennel before,' I said to him. 'Come on, I thought you would love it!' But he did not want to sleep so far away from me, and in the end he slept downstairs that night, on a cardboard box that he flattened when he settled down on it with a contented thump, as he always had done.

No one told me it was bedtime but eventually I went, unable to stop yawning. My mother sat on the side of my bed in the room I had been allowed to claim as my own, the one that looked down the drive. She had only a vest on and tracksuit bottoms, and her face and arms were clammy and hot. We could hear my father whistling in the courtyard and talking to Elijah.

'We're going to stay here, aren't we?' I said.

She smiled and said: 'I think we might.'

Beyond the lead of the window-pane a new moon was rising. It made dark wicker of the pine tree, illuminating each of the branches and, because of its brightness, warping them too.

'Mum,' I said. 'Which was it in Eden: the Tree of Life or the Tree of Knowledge?'

'The one Adam and Eve ate from?'

'Yes.'

'The Tree of Knowledge.'

'Oh.' I stretched my hand and touched the windowsill. 'Well then, maybe ours is the Tree of Life.'

'What d'you mean?'

'The pine tree in the garden.'

My mother bent and kissed me, a loud, boisterous smack, and I smiled at her.

'I'm going to find God here,' I said.

Her eyes became deep then and she kissed me quietly on my forehead, a kiss that whispered, a kiss to seal me up.

I woke that night many times and looked out at the moonlight flooding the courtyard like water. Unlike water, however, it didn't pool in hollow places but turned them into islands, dangerous and dark, yet no more substantial than holes cut in card, and the light that came through them was so bright that it hurt my eyes. What would it be like to live by such light always? To move always in this night? To look out at it was part horror, part wonder, and each time I meant to turn away I found I could not because I believed it contained a principle that applied to all things, and I felt that if I could just understand it, I would be at peace for the rest of my life. I wished I was older so that I could understand, though later on, when I was older, I knew I had never been closer to guessing it than I had been that night.

The next morning my parents slept in for the first time I could remember. I stood in the doorway of their bedroom, saw the sun falling across their vacant faces, then tiptoed down to the kitchen, hushed Elijah, who was bouncing on his front paws and whining, and let us out. I climbed the gate to the long field, Elijah going through it with a quick sideways flip, as if he had been slipping through five-bar gates all his life, and we stood in the grass. The land was glowing at the edges, catching light here and there as if someone were running with a burning branch and touching life into it. I felt that the morning was being presented to me, and each day, for quite a long time after that, waking up was like being given a gift that I tore open again and again. We each tore it in our different ways.

My father cleared the water-pump of slime and we cheered as water cascaded into the trough. He sharpened an old scythe and began cutting the grass. He worked all day while we trailed behind him, binding the grass in sheaves, hardly able to see for flies, and each evening, as the sun gilded the hummocky shape of the mountains, he walked around the perimeter of the garden. 'Look at the view! Smell that!' He pointed, he lifted a flower to his nose.

My mother and I followed, obedient, attentive. Then he sat, sipping cider. I was happy for my father, but he called the farm his estate and the garden his park; I resented the appropriation.

'It's all of ours,' I said to my mother. 'Isn't it?'

My mother and I cleaned the outbuildings, washed curtains, cupboards and floors. She gathered enormous bunches of flowers that she dried by hanging them from the beams in the kitchen. Each morning I washed in cold water, then took my breakfast into the garden and ate it beneath the tall pine. I walked in the fields, brushed my hands through the heads of the grass, broke my bread, sluiced my arms to the elbows and let the water dry on my skin. I chewed food more thoroughly than I had ever done before, till it was a fine paste, and walked around like a modern-day Crusoe with nothing on but my vest and dungarees, carrying a stick my father cut for me. These were the things the men of old did, I imagined (though not wear dungarees): the men who knew God. If God was to be found, then I was sure this was the place I would find Him.

I say some of this to Lucas, but not all.

'You mentioned feeling some frustration at your father's appropriation of the new house,' he says. 'How were relations generally between you at that time?'

I think for a moment. 'He said I'd grown taller. Sometimes I found him watching me.'

'Really?'

'As if I – as if I was a stranger.'

'Perhaps because you were becoming a woman.'

'I don't think so. We were just – more aware of each other.'

'Can you give me an example?'

'One night we chased horses that had broken into the garden.'

We were sitting down to our evening meal at the table, which we had moved into the kitchen, when we heard something pass through the courtyard like a freight train. The ground shook, the dinner plates rattled. Through the window we saw a stream of black and white and brown bodies. Elijah was barking excitedly by the front door. My father opened it and the courtyard was filled with milling horses, enormous beasts with god-like thighs, feathered hooves and rolling eyes. We could hear more, too, in the garden. My father shut the door and came back inside and grabbed two saucepans.

'We've got to stop them, they'll trample everything!' he yelled.

We stared at him, then something flared in our bodies like matches and we followed as he charged through the doorway, shouting and banging the pans.

We went right into the middle of the horses and the herd churned.

'Get them down the drive!' my father was shouting, his eyes as wild as the horses' themselves.

He ran around to the big gate and we heard him crashing through the undergrowth in the garden. Elijah had the time of his life, ducking and snapping at their hooves, driving the horses out from the sides of the courtyard, herding them into a riotous group. The horses clattered and surged, then picked up speed, thundering down the drive and shying left into the field at the gate that my father held open with a sheet of corrugated iron. We ran down to the bottom of the garden and pushed the corrugated sheets back into place and secured them with stones. We came back up to the house laughing, incredulous, exultant.

Lucas is frowning slightly, perhaps wanting something else. 'Were there any other "bonding" experiences?'

I shift in my seat.

'Anything at all you remember about your father and you?'

There is a long pause.

'One afternoon I helped my father in the garden. He was clearing the brambles and I helped him wheel them to the bonfire.'

'How did that feel?'

'I don't know . . . unusual.'

'In what way?'

'I don't know.'

'Can you tell me about it?'

The worst of this therapy is knowing Lucas will find out things I do not give him permission to while I am asleep.

I sigh. 'I really don't know – it was – it was like . . . well, almost as if we had been introduced to each other.'

'Introduced to each other?' He writes this down.

I remember the smell of my father that afternoon. It was acrid and thin, a sour smell, like I imagined an old woman would smell. He had never asked me to help him do anything. I put on the gloves he gave me and began hacking with the stick. Elijah sat on the grass to wait for me, chewing the underneath of his foot and wrinkling his nose like a mouse. The afternoon was cloudy and warm. Distances beckoned. There was an intimacy in our actions, a complicity neither my father nor I welcomed, but we bore with it nonetheless, an exchange of more than just briars. It was hard work, we panted, and afterwards we ached, but space was cleared. I was surprised at just how much.

We went back up to the house, Elijah bounding behind us, particularly playful now I was his again, pouncing on my feet, but just then I wished he wouldn't because I was trying to impress my father – as if I had just met him, as if he were a stranger – by a hundred little things: the way I swung my arms, the way I carried myself beside him, the small sniff I gave as we entered the courtyard: businesslike, workmanlike, slightly bored, adult.

I tell Lucas none of this. He looks up. 'And this experience made you feel closer to your father?'
'A bit.'
'Did anything else happen that afternoon?'
'No; not that I can remember.'

But it did, perhaps the most important thing of all. Inside the house my father said: 'Wait a minute, I've got something for you,' and he went into the front room and came back with a knife.
'Wow,' I said. 'Thanks.'
As I went forwards to take it, Elijah had hold of my laces and I stumbled. I kicked him away because he had made me seem like a fool in front of my father – whom I always felt something of a fool in front of, as if I could not do the smallest thing without mishandling it in some way – and he yelped. I took the knife. I knew I was flushing. The knife was cold in my hand and heavy. I remember thinking that it seemed to have already lived a long time,

much longer than me, and had done more things than I ever had. It had seven different blades and a red cross on the handle.

'Picked it up in an antique store on the quay,' my father said. 'It's a good one.' He'd meant to keep it, but I'd worked hard. 'Always cut away from yourself, see?' He showed me. 'And keep the blades turned in.'

'Thanks, Dad.'

'All right—'

It was enough already.

I went out into the garden and whistled for Elijah. He did not appear. The knife felt heavy and important in my pocket. I tried it out on the pine tree and it cut well, I hardly had to press down at all. I lifted the bark to my nose and smelt the tree's blood.

At dinner my mother was appalled.

'It's fine!' my father said. 'Quite safe; it's a Swiss army knife. Anyway,' he reached for the apple sauce. 'She can handle it.' He nodded in my direction (it was not an acknowledgment but as good as). 'She's a big girl, a country girl now.'

'Can we finish here?' I say. The painkillers are wearing off and sitting still is becoming difficult.

Lucas looks at me. 'I sense we're coming to something; are we?'

'No,' I say. 'Not that I know of.' I laugh quickly. 'But of course, you're the doctor.'

We look at each other.

'There's nothing more to tell!' I say. 'We went back to the house, my father said he was pleased with me.' I shrug.

'All right,' he says closing the notebook. 'Let's wrap it up for today. Good work, Madeline.'

The Price of Transgression

Lucas was sent to us. I heard it outside the meeting room today. I heard the words 'efficiency', 'targets', 'priority' and 'results'. In short it seems the powers that be deemed our little backwater in need of a shake-up and decided Lucas was the man for the job. When the door of the meeting room opened I pretended I was resting on a chair as I often do during my turns along the corridor. Sue, Margaret and Pete came out and went in the opposite direction without seeing me. I heard Margaret say: 'Well, if he wants twice the results he'll have to employ twice the manpower.'

After that the nurses from the other wards came out too and they all looked hot and dazed like Sue and Pete and Margaret, and it occurred to me, as it has before, that we patients might not be the only ones riding the shockwaves of the phenomenon known as S. Lucas. Since he arrived there has been meeting after meeting and I have heard the nurses complaining about the paperwork they have to take home.

However, while the nurses may be feeling the pressure it is in us patients that the effects are most readily visible. Our hour with Lucas is our day of reckoning, the time for personal interaction with the purveyor of our fates. The sinners are cast off to his left and the sheep are gathered to his right: sinners, in this case, meaning those who are failing to respond to Lucas's choice of therapy. The 'punish-ment' is generally an increase (or a decrease) in our medi-cation and additional therapy.

Some of us deal better with it than others. This afternoon

when I enter the lounge Brendan is sitting on the edge of the sofa, blinking, his face very white. Sue comes round with the tray of tablets but he won't take his beaker. Pete puts his hand on his shoulder and says: 'Take your tablets, Brendan, and then we'll put on the science programme you like.'

Brendan scratches his head hard and begins to rock. Pete moves towards him but he lashes out at him and rocks even faster.

I try to catch Brendan's eye but can't.

'Take your tablets, Brendan,' Pete says, but the beaker remains on the tray and the rocking continues.

Pete sits down gently beside Brendan, closes his hand around Brendan's and tries to open it to place the tablets in it. So much for Lucas's new rule, I think. Brendan starts to groan. The groaning gets louder.

Pete says: 'Brendan, stop playing now, take the tablets, there's a good man.'

Sue takes Robyn, who is also sitting on the sofa, by the arm and leads her to the other side of the room. She herds the rest of us over too. Then Pete takes hold of Brendan's arms while Sue picks up the beaker. The rocking persists for a split second. The next, the beaker's contents are flung skywards, Sue stumbles backwards, nursing her wrist, and Pete collides with the coffee table.

Then Brendan leaps up and begins to cry. Not 'cry' in the usual sense of the word, admittedly, but there are tears, and his face is contorted. The sound he makes, though, is not a spasmodic sobbing but an astonishing wail, a wail that makes me feel cold and reminds me of something I have heard before, a noise that grows as he raises himself on his toes and subsides as he descends, then continues monotonously with weird oblivion, self-sufficiency and abstraction, that makes me think not of a human weeping but an animal howling. I haven't heard Brendan make this noise in the five years he has been here; normally he makes no sound at all apart from the odd grunt. To see him cry, albeit in this unusual manner, is as shocking as if he had just come up to me, clapped me on the back and said: 'How are you, Madeline?' It is so shocking that my stomach lurches and for a moment I just stand there.

After she has collected herself, Sue says loudly: 'Brendan! Stop that! Come and sit down!'

Pete is saying: 'Come on, Brendan, there's a good man. Look, here's your book!'

But Brendan carries on making the piercing din.

I find myself walking towards him. My heart is beating hard and I don't know what I am going to do or even if I should try to do anything at all. I don't even mean to go up to him.

'Sit down, Madeline,' Sue says.

But I don't. I stand in front of Brendan and watch his chest swell and his arms strain. The noise is like a wall of water, but instead of trying to get it to stop I stand there and submit to it; I go along with it. I suppose I agree with it. It is immense. I seem to be tottering. My body is encased in heat. And then something strange is happening to me too. My own eyes are filling. It is as natural as falling asleep but strange too because I never cry. I keep listening, looking at him, my chest filling till it feels as if it will shatter, and Brendan keeps caterwauling and rising up on his toes.

Then without warning the noise stops, and he drops with a thud onto the sofa as if the strings that are holding him up have been cut, his arms still stiff at his sides. Sue stops shouting, Pete stops talking. Sue hovers but thinks better of speaking; Pete beckons to Mary who is sitting beside him to come away. Brendan sits staring at nothing, his mouth gaping, the same expression of horror on his face. I know he won't look at me but I think he knows I am present, I think he has become aware of me while he is crying because I have given him attention in a way that no one else has, so I stay where I am.

'D'you want your book, Brendan?' Pete says gently. He fetches *The Cosmological Principle*.

Brendan does not touch it. He carries on staring straight ahead. He appears to have fallen into a trance. After another few minutes of not wanting to see the expression of pain on his face any longer and feeling in rather a stupor myself, I go into the corridor and sit down on a chair. I feel as hollow as a stalk, as though all the fluid has been drained from my body.

A few minutes later I hear a voice say: 'What's the matter?' and look up to see Sue's sharp face.

'I don't feel well,' I say. I wish she would leave. Then I say: 'What's the matter with Brendan? I've never seen him like that.'

'There's nothing the matter with him,' Sue says. 'Dr Lucas's changed his medication, that's all; he's just having a grizzle. He'll be fine in a week.' She looks cross, whether with me or with Brendan or with Dr Lucas, I don't know.

'A grizzle?' I say. 'He was howling; Brendan never makes a sound.'

'Brendan is fine, Madeline. Why don't you go and watch telly?' she says. 'It'll be time for your meds soon.' She turns on her heel and sets off down the corridor. I watch her sensible shoes retreat.

For the rest of the afternoon, as Pam sucks her string and twists it, as Miriam builds a castle of red blocks and claims they are yellow, as Eugene walks back and forth, hands in pockets, murmuring Latin, and Margaret strokes Robyn's scalp with a knitting needle, I think of Brendan and those unearthly cries.

Just before bedtime I realise where I have heard them before: on a misty day at the farm when from my bedroom I heard a hunt and the sound of a fox. My mother said:

'Foxes are terrible; they kill far more than they need to.' It did not make me feel better. I remember what my father told me: that no debt is repaid once but many times over, and the price for transgression can as easily be too high as too low.

The Journal

'What have you done to Brendan?' I say. I know I shouldn't have. It does not do to get overheated. Only amenable patients are candidates for release. Gods must be propitiated or they get sulky, the sky clouds over and the land becomes dark – but then I see him, with his shiny shoes, his perfect hair, his impeccable suit.

'Why d'you say that, Madeline?' Lucas says calmly.

'He cried!' I say. 'Brendan *never* cries.'

'Brendan is a little unstable at the moment due to a modification of his treatment,' he says. 'But it's nothing for you to be concerned about.'

'Well, I am!' I say. 'Whether I should or I shouldn't be – I am concerned!'

Lucas smiles. 'And I'm glad to see that, Madeline, it's a very encouraging sign.'

'This isn't about *me*!' I say.

'But that's where you're wrong, Madeline,' he says. 'This *is* about you; this is your session. And I'm afraid I can't talk about Brendan during it.'

I open my mouth.

'Like yourself,' he says, 'Brendan has been the subject of misguided treatment. I am simply adjusting it.'

I think of many rejoinders, but I do not voice any of them, only sit, feeling very hot, and mutter again: 'I've never seen Brendan like that – and I've known him five years.'

'Okay,' he says, with a note of finality. 'I can't talk about Brendan with you. His case is private, as is yours. Now is there anything else you wanted to ask me before we begin?'

'Yes,' I say. 'There is something. The programme – *my* programme: I don't think it's working.'

'Oh?' He raises his eyebrows. I hate it when he pretends to accommodate me, when he personifies patience.

'I'm not getting stronger, I'm getting weaker. I'm sleeping less, I'm *much* more anxious, I feel sick pretty much constantly and some days the exhaustion makes it almost impossible to get up.'

'Anything else?'

I stare at him.

'Now, Madeline,' he leans backwards and interlaces his fingers. 'Do you remember I told you when we started that it wouldn't be easy?' He holds up his hand. 'Wait – that you would have to bear with it?' He pauses, presumably to let his words sink in because as I open my mouth he begins to speak again. 'Now I'll ask you a question: do you believe I have your best interests at heart?'

My heart beats strangely and I look away.

'Don't you think I've seen other patients struggle like you? It's true you're finding things difficult, it's true you're more anxious, but as far as I'm concerned these are positive signs; they mean you're progressing. As regards the fatigue, Graded Exercise and CBT are both proven ways to treat it; it can take some people some time before they see any improvement.'

'But I'm going backwards!' I say. 'I'm not even remaining stationary!'

'You're progressing, Madeline,' he says. 'You're progressing in leaps and bounds!'

I stare at him.

'A great many of you are progressing, however it may appear on the surface.'

Is that possible? I let myself consider this a moment.

He rotates in the chair and inhales as if weary.

'Madeline,' he says, 'real healing always makes the

situation appear worse for a little while; it's a well-known concept in the East. Real healing initially appears to be doing the opposite to what you think it should do. It's the same with memory: the trick to recovering something – anything at all – is to look the other way, to act as if you never lost it. The less you pursue a thing the more likely it is to come to you. It's like catching a wild animal. At the moment we're not going to the heart of the matter, we're concentrating on other ways of facilitating recall. And to that end, for the next few weeks I'd like you to immerse yourself as much as possible in those first months at the farm; I'd like you to bring your journal next time and, before you do, look over it.'

My stomach lurches and I stare at him. All thought of Brendan is momentarily forgotten. How did Lucas know about the journal? Were my possessions *logged* somewhere? But of course they are. In any case, he does know.

'Will you do that?'

'Yes,' I say faintly. What else can I say?

'By the way, I was quite impressed with the journal,' he says. 'I would say that at the farm you underwent a conversion experience; some of the entries are astonishing, epiphanic, extraordinarily intense. Rereading them is your homework this week; I want you to remember what it felt like to be that thirteen-year-old girl – it's vitally important. All right?'

I say nothing.

'All right? Madeline?'

'All right,' I say. I want to go. I want to curl up, bury myself in darkness. I want to be covered over.

I want to rage, I want to weep, I want to retch. But most of all I want to sleep.

It is a small book bound with string. The spine is split, the cover brown, wound with sellotape that is now flaking and yellow. Inside, stuck or pasted or pressed, there are leaves and flowers, dragonfly wings, sap stains, pollen, holly, dried berries, an empty chrysalis, a buttercup. On one page there is something that looks like blood, on another a brown smudge with green particles beneath the sellotape, which I see on looking closer and reading the entry is mussel soup. I lift the book to my nose but it is as scentless as a bone. There are three photographs: one of a woman in an apple tree wearing a coat that has emulsion paint on it; another of a man holding up sticks of giant rhubarb; another of a girl with her arms around a black-and-white dog. Everywhere there is very small, very crowded writing, an attempt to make the writing illegible to anyone but the author herself.

On four pages there are no words at all. On the first there is a drawn map of the farm; on the second there is a drawing of a mouse; on the third a drawing of a bird. The last page of the four is coloured in black with a biro, so that when the light shines upon it, it is a dull red. The first pages of the journal are taken up with lists. This is the first entry:

This is the journal of my fourteenth year. It hasn't really begun yet but I already know it will be the best year of my life. My task this year is to find You. The blazing arc of the sky tells me it is possible, the hills say it too, the fields swallowed up in the afternoon sun nod their heads. I step off into the arms of the air . . .

I turn over the page.

There are days here when the wind comes scudding across the fields and sap runs dark from the silver birches and glistens like snakes and a chord chimes deep in the earth. I think then that Your breath is in the wind and the fields are rooms in Your house and when I sit You have said: 'Pull up a chair,' and when I lie in the grass You cover me over. There are days here that feel like years, there are whole afternoons that pass by like dreams, there are hours on end when I can think nothing at all.

You can stack these things up, you can press them together, something will come of it.

'How much of it did you manage to read?'

'The opening pages.'

'You have to read more, all right?'

He is flicking through the journal. The sight of his hands touching it makes me feel nauseous. I turn and look out of the window where I can see the horse-chestnut trees. It is sunny today, for the first time in ages, and Lethem Park has been transformed. It is hard to believe I might be free to walk where I want to soon. This is not an idle dream; he has said I am progressing. He has said the word 'rehabilitation' more than once. He has said: 'distinct possibility'. I have not thought what I would do if I was released, partly for fear of destroying the possibility. I know that for some time I would be in secure accommodation, a sort of halfway house between this world and the next, but after that I don't know. I have wondered whether I would be well enough to live alone. I believe that my illness would subside dramatically if I was no longer here – Lucas believes it is psychosomatic in any case, and if Lucas and I have unearthed the psychic stuff, then what will there be to stop me functioning as well as any other person?

He says: 'What's this?'

'A mouse,' I say – or think I do. I swallow.

'Yes, I can see it's a mouse. Why is it filling the whole page?'

I shrug.

'There's another drawing further on of a bird. Did you draw them for any particular reason?'

'No – I don't know; I can't remember.'

'And what's this?'

I look up again. I look away. 'The Ark of the Covenant.'

'I'm sorry?'

'The Ark of the Covenant.'

'The wooden chest that contained the tablets of the law? The one the Israelites carried through the wilderness?'

'Yes,' I say quietly.

Lucas frowns. 'Before we go any further, why don't you tell me a little bit more about your beliefs, Madeline – or your father's beliefs.'

'Where do you want me to begin?'

'The core tenets?'

'Well . . . faith in Christ's sacrifice . . . sin . . . redemption.'

'Standard Christianity.'

'More or less.'

I hear his pencil scratching in the notebook. The lead is so sharp it makes a rasping sound. 'Did you believe in the Old Testament too?'

'Oh yes,' I say. 'The foundation of our faith really was the life-for-a-life principle or the Mosaic law: blood sacrifice, which itself formed the basis of Christ's own sacrifice of his human life,' I say.

'Blood sacrifice?'

'Blood was sacred,' I say. 'It contained the life and so belonged to God.'

I am hot and my muscles are beginning to feel nauseated, a sensation I have tried to describe to various doctors. I wrap my arms around my chest in an attempt to wrest the sickness out of them; sometimes holding them tightly like this dissipates the feeling.

'The law requires nearly everything to be cleansed with blood, and without the shedding of blood no forgiveness takes place.'

'Is that taken from a particular verse?' he says. 'It sounds like—'

'Hebrews, chapter nine, verse twenty-two.'

'That's the New Testament.'

'Yes, but the principle of a life given to buy back life runs through the whole bible; Christ's crucifixion was a blood sacrifice. For all mankind.'

He inhales, frowning. 'And was that what God was like to you? An Old Testament God of vengeance and retribution? Or was He a New Testament God of forgiveness and love? I know He was very real to you, obviously, because half your journal entries are addressed to Him, but how did you see Him?'

I suddenly notice I am breathing heavily. I attempt to do so less audibly. 'Both,' I say, 'all of those things. At different times.'

He turns a few more pages and raises his eyebrows. 'Where were you when you drew *this*?' He holds up the page on which I drew the map of the farm.

'In the hayloft,' I say. 'There was a small yard bordering our land, with some run-down sheds and a hayloft. I climbed up to the top of the bales.'

'It's incredibly detailed . . .' He turns the page, then puts the journal aside. 'You sold the farm quickly, didn't you?'

'Yes. Well . . . it was hardly a sale at all, really, more of a handover.'

He looks up. 'Do you think your father would have sold it even if everything had gone according to plan?'

It is quite a long time before I answer. 'No. He intended – we intended – to stay there forever.'

'And do you think you ran away because you couldn't accept what was happening to your mother?'

'I don't know,' I say, and suddenly the sickness in my limbs is too much. 'Can we finish here?'

But he is saying: 'You see' — he puts his fingers to his lips — 'I thought you would have been anxious to stay with her, not run away. There's something there that isn't quite right. There's something I'm missing. In most cases the primary cause of dissociative amnesia is some sort of trauma. In your case the psychosocial environment is massively conflictual — there must have been dozens of uncomfortable emotions and impulses you were feeling.'

'I don't know—'

'Well, I know you don't remember feeling them now, but here in the journal there are some very agitated entries. Can you remember experiencing some of those emotions?'

'I remember being angry at my father,' I say.

'And for you and your father, anger is a sin,' he says. 'And do you think he was ever aware of your feelings towards him?'

'I don't know.'

'And were there any sexual compulsions?'

'No—!'

'You were very isolated, Madeline. You didn't even have any other children to bounce things off . . . The religious dynamic meant that sex was probably viewed in a very delimiting light; it would have been natural to feel uneasy about sexual matters as you reached puberty with no one to talk to.'

'No. It was all totally — of no interest to me.'

'Are you sure there aren't any feelings that troubled you?'

'Not that I can remember.'

'A lot of forgetting there—'

'I didn't even know what sex was,' I say, then wish that I hadn't.

'Then when did you find out?'

'Afterwards . . .' I close my eyes. 'I *need* to finish now.'

He inhales and then gets up. 'Bring the journal again

next week. I'll expect you to have read more. Don't think it's unimportant. Remember what we're working towards here.'

'I do,' I say. This is one thing I have not forgotten.

Journal II

I can hear the central heating and Pam snoring and the night nurses talking in the corridor. Moonlight is filling the room. I bring a chair to the window; turning on the light will only arouse suspicion and I do not want to be disturbed. On my lap lies the journal. It's just words, I say to myself. How bad can words be?

This is the journal of my fourteenth year. It hasn't really begun yet but I already know it will be the best year of my life. My task this year is to find You. The blazing arc of the sky tells me it is possible, the hills say it too, the fields swallowed up in the afternoon sun nod their heads. I step off into the arms of the air . . .

. . . If everything in the world was offered to me I would not exchange it for an hour here or a day, though there is no time here and no hour but now. The days are a pendulum, swinging back to where they began, repeating endlessly, never done. There is no choosing here, one thing over another. It isn't 'either/or', or 'instead of'. It is all things always, all things one . . .

. . . When You made the world You must have decreed there be a little more light here than anywhere else. The light here erases me. Each day I ask the light to erase me a little bit more. I have asked my mother if you can be blinded by sunlight.

I wake to light and go to sleep in it.

The trees are misted in green, the earth is trickling and

rushing, the land is being born again but we are still locked in the cold. Why do You come to me, God, yet punish us too? . . .

. . . The rope spun past the numbers at our feet. I banished them to infinity. There was fire in me, I was writing a word, tracing dark letters on the light . . .

. . . Halfway down the lane I saw her and Elijah coming towards me. Elijah raced up, bending his body and groaning in happiness, then ran back to Mum, as if wanting to bring us together. I ran up to her and hugged her so hard . . .

. . . God in heaven, forgive me. Forgive me . . .

. . . – and right down in the hollows of the trees, in the roots and the cracks and the crannies; in each cleft and clump, the coloured mosses and the ribbons of fungi and bright coloured beetles and bugs – there is light. And each blade and each leaf and each tree is illuminated.

Journal III

The moon is here again. It is blazing like fire along the sheets and pillows, lighting the wall behind me, filling my eyes and my ears until sleep has gone; it is as if the moon wants me to read. I get up, take the journal and sit in the chair by the window.

I have asked my mother if you can be blinded by sunlight.

Trees are alive – and they are bigger than people think.

Elijah and I made a house . . .

I begin to cry.
'Keep going,' says a voice.

I have found God.

We have cut down the big pine.

'It's no good,' I say.
'Keep going,' says the voice. I think it is the moon.

What does it mean to be sorry?

. . . without blood it is impossible.

I am going to save her.

I lean my head against the wall. 'I can't,' I say.
'You can,' says the moon, 'and when you have, you will see me face to face.'
I shake my head. 'It's too difficult.' Even breathing is

difficult now, as if my chest has been laced up too tightly and cannot expand.

'If you do this you will be free,' says the moon.

I get up. I walk one way and then the other. I press my forehead against the wall and close my eyes. But then I go back to the chair and open the journal, and this time I do not get up.

LEVITICUS

*

Lethem Park Mental Infirmary
April 2010

Blades of Grass

13 June

Dear God,

This is the journal of my fourteenth year. It hasn't really begun yet but I already know it will be the best year of my life. My task this year is to find You. The blazing arc of the sky tells me it is possible, the hills say it too, the fields swallowed up in the afternoon sun nod their heads. I step off into the arms of the air.

I don't know how long I wanted to find You – a long, long time. Something in the light here says that I might. It's wild, it comes from beyond the rim of the world, and the world is new and I feel a tugging in the pit of my stomach I can't find a place for.

We have come to this place that it seems to me You have made for us. We were obedient so You remembered us. You remembered Your covenant.

If You come to me I will be ready, I will do whatever You ask. You will not have to ask twice, You will not have to remind me.

22 June

Dear God,

Elijah and I go into the fields and it is like I am seeing things for the first time. I don't know names any more, I just see shapes and colours.

In the mornings I wash in cold water. I take my breakfast into the garden. I don't eat indoors any more.

I read my bible and think about the words till they are like pebbles on my tongue. All around me the garden rustles and sways. It watches, it tries to distract me. As I look at it, green becomes greener, the flowers glow like little lights. Who knew flowers could do that?

At night when I take off my clothes there are seeds in my socks, there are stains on my knees, my nails have soil beneath them and my hair smells of sky.

9 July

Dear God,

I know which shoots in the hedges are good to eat now. There are some that are sweet and some hot like pepper. I see when it is going to rain and what the clouds are called. My skin is changing, my eyes are becoming clearer. It feels like my heart has stopped and started again and is beating with a new rhythm. My lungs have become bigger, I can feel them stretching. My legs and arms are becoming strong. Soon there will be nothing left of who I was.

10 July

Dear God,

We go walking, Elijah and I. Often we run. The land opens out beneath us. Wherever we run, there it is, and wherever we don't, there it is not. It is as if we are creating it, moment by moment. We stay out till it gets dark and the chill winds come.

11 July

Dear God,

There is so much light here! Sometimes I can't see the road for it. When You made the world You must have decreed there be a little more light here than anywhere else. The light here erases me. Each day I ask the light to erase me a little bit more.

When we come in at night the light is in my face and in Elijah's fur, you can smell it, and I am full, as if I have drunk the light up. I am full and yet I'm weightless. My arms and legs are heavy but I am as scattered and insubstantial as air, as chaff, as the water drops from the pump in the yard. I feel I have been breathed in and out by something much bigger than me. I have asked my mother if you can be blinded by sunlight.

I wake to light and go to sleep in it.

24 July

Dear God,

There is a place on the earth where I sit, at the base of the oak tree in the long field, and it feels as if I am at the centre of everything, of all time too, and I am nowhere, but somewhere better than anywhere else.

In the long field Elijah and I lie down and the grass covers us. The grass feels warm and busy. When the wind moves it I feel it is talking to me. I remember the verse about the Holy Spirit moving through the upper room like a stiff rushing breeze, giving the apostles the tongues of the spirit. If the grass is filled with Your spirit I speak its language. The grass says 'always', the grass says 'now'. Each blade is the same but it is different. Each blade has an eye. I pass through the eyes and see a world in each one.

The grasses talk and they sing and they look out. And the grasses cut, God, they cut deeply.

26 July

Dear God,

I will find You, I'm sure, it's just a matter of time. Each day I try to get beneath things. I wear almost nothing, my dungarees sometimes, that's all. My skin is the only thing between us now. I feel the earth with my feet, with my hands and my knees. I press my cheek to the soil. I run my hands over things – the trunk of the big pine, the horseshoe above the barn door, the place where the water comes through the pump, the granite millstone with the red streak of rust. I'm printing myself here, planting myself, building up a record. I am a blind person learning to read and a deaf person beginning to hear and a lame person learning to walk. I am dumb, making words with whatever I find.

I am waking. I wake again and again.

28 July

Dear God,

In the long afternoons Elijah and I lie in the garden and I don't know whether the house is travelling or the clouds, I don't know whether the earth is pulsing or the palms of my hands. I look at the sky so long I think it might be the whites of my eyes and the clouds are the spaces inside me. I am gone, I am nowhere, nothing at all, a hole in the fabric of things.

If I lie still long enough my body feels part of the ground. I go away and someone else comes. I don't know whether I am sleeping or awake and when I get up my head is as light as a dandelion clock but my stomach is full.

I have eaten grass and tasted the soil.

30 July

Dear God,

I see trees now and know I never saw a tree before, just cut-out things that were flat and lifeless. Trees are as alive as people are! I feel bad that I ever cut the pine tree with my knife. Trees are alive – and they are bigger than *people think. There is a halo that surrounds them. If you wait long enough the real trees come out. I showed Mum how I can close my eyes and walk amongst them without bumping into them.*

Tonight I heard her ask my father if I should have company.

4 *August*

Dear God,

There are days here when the wind comes scudding across the fields and sap runs dark from the silver birches and glistens like snakes and a chord chimes deep in the earth. I think then that Your breath is in the wind and the fields are rooms in Your house and when I sit You have said: 'Pull up a chair,' and when I lie in the grass You cover me over. There are days here that feel like years, there are whole afternoons that pass by like dreams, there are hours on end when I can think nothing at all.

You can stack these things up, you can press them together, something will come of it.

7 *August*

Dear God,

There is a feeling that comes over me in bed, something passes through me like a current and I feel myself humming. I knew where we were the minute we arrived. I remembered. This land is old land, it was promised to us, and now it is ours.

8 *August*

Dear God,

If everything in the world was offered to me I would not exchange it for an hour here or a day, though there is no time here and no hour but now. The days are a pendulum, swinging back to where they began, repeating endlessly, never done. There is no choosing here, of one thing over another. It isn't 'either/or', or 'instead of'. It is all things always, all things one.

The Ability to Choose

Memory is a strange thing. It doesn't always retain what we think it will. For instance, I can clearly remember the crack that appeared in the kitchen ceiling the night my father knocked his head on the lintel. It spread from the lintel to the stairs in the corner. But I remember nothing about my mother's face the last time I saw her. I can remember the smell of the mussel soup she made the evening my father found work but not how the farm looked the night I ran away.

Last night I was wandering again. 'Wandering' is the word I use. 'Walking' suggests something purposeful and I have nowhere to go, though I look about me, which suggests I am expecting to find something. I am in a lane. It is early autumn, the afternoon is warm, the land lying in a comfortable torpor beneath grey skies. The breeze carries a smell of silage. I have the impression there are great distances either side of me beyond the hedge. The light is bright for the time of day and as I continue along the lane it seems to brighten still further, the sun a white aureole in a heavy bank of cloud. The road rises. A conglomeration of trees on the brow of a hill look familiar. I quicken my pace. A track turns to the left and appears to lead upwards. I begin to run. But the road slopes away, the trees are different, the track is not the same and I must go on again.

I am in a field. It is summer and I am sunburnt and find comfort in the greenness and moisture. The field leads down to a river. It is all rather ghostly. The place has its own sun and its own stars. White flowers border the banks. They are paler than the irises that lined the river at the farm, tall and fleshy, an absence of colour in the green that surrounds them, small apertures. The flowers seem to be in mourning but I do not know for what. I slip in amongst them.

I could stay here for ever. I could be happy here at the end of all things. There is no more searching, no more arriving or departing, no more longing, no more home – the very notion of home is meaningless here, as is that of time; before and after, here, there. I wade deeper amongst the long stems. I am tempted to eat the flowers and I know that if I did they would taste like honey and wild bitter-sweetness; as I approach the bank I am tempted to lap the river and I know that if I did it would taste intimate and holy, of saliva and soul.

I take my shoes and socks off and sit on the edge of the bank. In a while I might take a swim. Or I might stay here amongst the flowers and watch the river flow past. The pleasure lies in the ability to choose: I can wade in and let the water bear me up, or stay here for all time without so much as dipping my toe.

The Root of it All

My father said that one sin was the most insidious of all. There were many names for it: 'uncleanness' was one; 'immorality' another; 'the root of it all' was a third. His favourite, however, was 'unnatural desire', which posed the question whether it was the desire itself that was the problem or only the type – and how you could tell the difference, I never knew. An earthquake is natural though it swallows a town, a pig though she eats her own piglets, a whale when it skins a seal as it tosses it in midair. 'The root of it all' suggested it was precisely because the desire was natural that it was dangerous, being not only innate – and hence surely irreproachable – but insidious and hidden from view; extensive, encompassing everything, yet couched in obscurity.

The girl that discovered the root of it all is not with me any more. These are not her calves, her belly, her breasts, her skin, her eyes. Her skin is smooth and flushed, freckled with sunlight. Her legs are strong, her knees grubby, her body scentless except for the scent of childhood, subtle as the smell of grass or a dog's fur in the sun. Her breasts are not breasts but tender swellings, her body does not have hair but the merest coat of down. It is hard to believe I was her. Perhaps that is why I don't look at those parts of myself any more though an arrow of hair points the way; I know from experience that signposts can be misleading.

I just caught the smell of the girl then: mealy, faintly grimy. I have been remembering her smell more and more.

She and I are definitely strangers; I smell of sanitization, sometimes perspiration, and once a month menstrual blood. One day I will not even smell of that. I will smell of old age, a soothing smell, faintly sickly, reminiscent of infancy, with its potions and lotions and talcum powder. Then I suppose for a brief time I will smell of death, the final smell of all.

I still look a little like the girl. I have that dreaded virginal air about me. My gait is unworldly, disgustingly modest, and there is no point in make-up here. My hair is too shiny, too unadulterated, my skin perversely smooth, unmarked by life, by lust, by pollution, by stress, by child-birth or sunlight, and my clothes are those of the retarded: thick, long-sleeved, high-necked, knee-length, ankle-length; trainers, laced shoes. I used to loathe clothes and wanted nothing more than to tear them off; now, despite their ugliness, I cannot be parted from them. It was a question of skin – or perhaps of clothes – that started it all.

I was determined that we would keep the farm, that I – single-handedly, if necessary – would make God favour us, rain down blessings, keep us from harm. I prayed almost constantly, carried my pocket bible everywhere, recited psalms, and continually examined my thoughts to see whether they befitted a servant of God. Two weeks after we moved to the farm God apparently rewarded my efforts and brought my father work the other side of the island, helping to build a lifeboat house. With the first money he managed to save my father bought another car, a classic car, and one in such bad repair that the door fell off two days after he brought us home in it, and because he could not afford to get it fixed, it sat in the courtyard.

'What was wrong with our old car?' my mother said.

But there was never a good reason for any of the cars my father bought – and invariably sold at a loss, some time later.

With my father in work, my mother and I did not leave the farm for weeks except when we went with him to the supermarket on Friday nights. I didn't mind – at least I didn't think I did; I made a lookout tower upstairs in the dairy from which I could see the drive and at the first sound of wheels on the track Elijah and I ran to the bottom of the garden, Elijah bounding over the grass with his ears pricked as if it was a game. It was and it wasn't. The challenge was to get to the stream by the time tyres crackled over the courtyard gravel. It was only ever the postman, but I waited, heart pounding, until I heard the car door slam and the engine start up again. I knew there was something wrong with me; the children on the quay had taught me that. The less people saw me, the better. One evening I heard children in the field next to our garden. I watched them play tag for hours through the hedge, not making a sound, until I was stiff and cold.

In spite of my father's belief that people were the reason for my mother's depressions, I think my mother did mind the lack of contact. In the mornings she gave me lessons at the kitchen table. Neither of us wanted to do school-work but if we gave up we both felt guilty. In the afternoon she busied herself around the house or garden. Sometimes when she was supposed to be doing something I found her looking at nothing. If she saw me she nodded, tapping something as if she had just made a decision, then returned to making curtains or weeding the herb garden or planting vegetables or making tea. Once I saw her standing at the gate at the top of the drive, just standing there, not leaning on it or shading her eyes, her face blank, her arms at her sides. When she saw me she jumped, then laughed, put her arm around me and we walked back to the house. Then there was the afternoon when I came in from the fields to find the kitchen dark and empty. I climbed the stairs to see her sitting on her bed, her palms turned upwards in her lap. Several minutes went by and she did not move. Then my father's car pulled into the courtyard and she blinked and got up.

On one occasion she decided the two of us were going out.

'Where?' I said.

'To town.'

We locked Elijah in the kennel, where he whined pitifully, and got the bikes out of the shed. I asked if we could bring him and tie his leash to my handlebars but she said it wouldn't be safe. We set off singing as loudly as we could. We laughed and sang until we reached the top of a steep hill just outside town, then my mother's feet started to turn the pedals more slowly until finally she gently toppled sideways into the hedge. We walked the rest of the way and she couldn't sing any more because she was tired. Once we got into town she went straight to a café and ordered two cheeseburgers with fries and cokes.

'What are you doing?' I said.

'You've got to live a bit, love,' she said.

'Can we afford it?'

'I've got a secret hoard.'

I doubted this; my mother could hardly save anything from the housekeeping and there was no other source of money. The cokes trembled as she took the tray. She couldn't pierce her can so I did it for her; she had never had fries and wondered where the vinegar was. We held hands across the table and felt like children on an adventure. Anything was possible that day. We bought a disposable camera, some carrot seeds and two cheap tennis rackets, then rode home. A long line of cars built up behind us, going up the hill out of town; my mother fell into the hedge again and we walked half the way back.

We went into town three more times and then stopped going. I wasn't sorry; it felt dangerous, what we were doing. I hated the evasive answers at dinner when my father asked: 'What did you do today?' but my mother seemed to feel the loss. In the coming weeks she and I made excursions: to a wood to pick mushrooms, to fetch milk from a garage two miles away, to find a cove upstream where we picnicked. The journey was always more important to my mother than what we had to do there, and the length of it mattered more than our arrival.

God had blessed us, but I still had not found Him. I thought I had come close; all I needed was a little more intimate knowledge, a more personal proof. I searched for God in the fields and the woods but it was in the river I found Him, on a day of astonishing heat, when the light was strange and there was a void at the centre of things.

Those first months were hot, people remarked on it. In the town holidaymakers fanned themselves at pavement cafés. The beach, when we drove past it one day – broad and golden, with high sand dunes rounding to the Head – was teeming with people. My father came home from work with his arms and hands so freckled you could hardly see the white parts. In the house even opening the windows did not bring in the breeze. My mother and I walked barefoot. Elijah got up only to gulp noisily from his water bowl, then flopped back down in the shade. Before the dew had dried each morning, the sun appeared to be pulsing. Small breezes faltered and expired. The horizon was hazy, the ground scorching. Only late in the day did the heat lessen a little, shadows ticking by at the base of the pine as the sun slipped lower, warmed lips and eyes, flared sudden through apple tree boughs, lit grasses and leaves and dragonfly wings, as if concealed within each was a living coal, and veins held not sap but blood; skeins of jewel and flame. The moment the sun sank quivering into the earth was an incarnation and things toppled backwards, laid low by its might. Wherever it is now, the light passes still, gilding the river that widens and quickens away from the fields and the hills, past the tower and the bridge and the town on to the quay, to the lip of the sea, to the point called The Head, where the currents run deep, and woods cling to soil that is sand, and silt rich with rain.

I wouldn't have gone down to the river if it hadn't been for the heat, but neither would I have gone down to the river if they hadn't warned me not to. I could climb trees, walk the lanes, sit in the hayloft, sleep out in the garden or upstairs in the dairy, but the river was forbidden. It wasn't that easy to ignore, though. You could see it through the gap in the hedge at the bottom of the garden that was flanked by the sign warning trespassers – whether to stay in or keep out, I still wasn't sure. When the sun shone, light glanced off the water; in the rain we could hear its voice.

I was reminded of the river also because the garden itself was a source of some fascination. Creatures lurked there, leaves were shiny as if polished, colours richer than usual, so that they appeared almost luminous – yet in other places were darker than you would think they should be. There were box hedges that resembled humans and animals as clouds seem to do, and like clouds seemed to change imperceptibly in the time it took to look away and look back. There was an ancient schema palpable beneath your feet despite the long grass and the moss, its random shapes suggesting terraces and avenues, stones sleeping like the bones of a Babylon or an Atlantis.

There were other things that seemed to have no business in the garden at all: palms, tropical plants, large-leaved and glossy, flowers we did not know the names of, the strange flesh-coloured orchids that smelt like the dead animals I had seen sometimes at the side of the road, attracting hundreds of flies. The orchids suggested things about the earth here, uncomfortable things, particularly in view of what we knew about the previous inhabitant: that nothing ever really vanished but only seemed to, and could not be forgotten for it was bound to reappear.

What was most peculiar about the garden, however, was the conviction I had that I was being watched. I thought I caught the watcher occasionally in a shift of the treetops, in the movement they made before the wind came, but I couldn't make out the watcher's attitude. I didn't know whether it was amused, or curious, or something darker; I remembered the vagrant's words, and wondered once again whether the previous owner had killed himself in the garden. Odder still was that the experience of being watched was one of unease and, at the same time, familiarity, as if I had spent months in a room with a stranger but never been introduced. Was my uneasiness with myself or that which surrounded me, I asked myself. My father had said gods lived in this land. Was this why I felt so unsettled? Was it *their* bones I felt beneath my feet? Did their presence in the streams, the trees, the rocks, account for the certainty that I was being watched?

Elijah noticed it too. He would look around or sniff the air. Sometimes his hackles rose. Often the sensation was so strong that I turned, only to confront a tree or a flower, alarm spiking my scalp. That summer it occurred to me that the reason the first humans clothed themselves may well have been to shield themselves from such relentless curiosity, because in the garden I was made aware that what set me apart from my surroundings was my skin: it made me an object of alienation, of danger and perhaps of regret. Acute bodily discomfort prompted me to attempt to escape from my skin that fateful afternoon, dislodging the warning to trespassers at the bottom of the garden and stealing down to the river beyond.

On the afternoon I went down to the river we had been battling Newton's Third Law. My mother and I had missed lessons earlier and were making up for it later. But all I was conscious of was the sunlight falling across the kitchen table. It came in through the open front door, it flowed down each step of the stairs, making the banisters stand up like rotten teeth and the understairs black. It made aureoles of our hair and wiped out our hands and our faces. The light seemed too dense to simply be sunlight. The courtyard was erased, overexposed, bleached as white as marrow, as albumen, as skin without blood. Corners hoarded darkness as the ground hoards water in a drought. Against this whiteness objects appeared to be etched out; the shed doorways, the shadows cast by walls and trees and stones, had eaten away the blankness by means of some sort of acid. The light made other things seem imperfect. I closed my eyes against its brightness but all that happened was that the world appeared red-hot and in negative.

Through the open door where Elijah lay, a breeze carried a sweet scent of dung. Distances lapped at the house like water, but in the kitchen there was only the stale smell of baking and yellowing linoleum, motes in the air, a sill spotted with spider-blood. A tap dripped, the clock shaped like a saucepan ticked, Elijah yawned piercingly, mournfully, then went back to panting. When I looked at my mother her hand had opened gently, her head was on her arms and her eyes were shut.

Sweat slipped in rivulets down my back and pricked my scalp. The crotch of my dungarees chafed. My feet stuck to the cross-bar of the table, a rash I had developed on my stomach begged to be scratched. My body had been making its presence felt more and more lately. There were stirrings, wetness, vague pains low down. My breasts were swollen and tender; when I inspected them they looked angry. The graze of cotton across my nipples was painful and to touch them was half sickness, half pleasure, the sensation drawing me towards something. Were these changes evidence of God, I wondered? Was this awakening? Hadn't I prayed to be wakened?

That afternoon I tried to go back to Newton, but the light blotted out the words, made the pencil slide between my finger and thumb, my brain turn to felt. My mother's mouth gaped a little wider. Her cheeks were flushed. I could see the dark whorl of hair at her crown. Her mouth furled and slackened, with a soft pock; ffff . . . pock; ffff . . . pock; ffff . . . A space opened between the rise and fall of her chest.

I put back the chair and crept to the door. Elijah jumped up and capered around me, groaning and twisting with delight.

'Shhhh,' I said, and we slipped out.

We went through the ivy-covered archway, past the orchard, the pine tree, the brambles, the stream. The sun on my head made me stumble. A strange pulse beat low in my body. Elijah was silent, running fast and low through the grass. We squeezed through the hedge and then we were racing, the fields spread out, the sky the colour of blue ink.

The river glittered like hot metal but freshness came up from it like a smell. Its voice was deep-throated and mellow, and the shade of the trees along the bank was a cool palm on my head. There were irises growing down by the river, great clumps of white heads standing taller than my waist, and when I waded in amongst them they towered into blue-black skies. That night when I went back to the farm with sunburn and freckles, and lay awake in the dark with the heat in my head and that other new place, and wondered whether what had happened was because of those flowers and those skies.

I tore off my clothes and slipped in where the irises grew thickest. The water was cold at first and then it was cool; it held you still if you pedalled against it and swept you away with infinite ease if you didn't. I played in the shallows but after a while I went to the deeps and hung there for hours while sound turned to silence and shivering to heat.

I cannot describe how good the water felt. The burden of my skin was instantly lighter. Mud billowed between my toes in mushroom clouds, pond-skaters dimpled the light on the surface, dragonflies hovered. I floated, the engorged sun tickling my eyelids, teasing them into an ecstasy of honeyed somnolence, till tears slipped from the corners, and when I opened them the fields had been changed to purple and blue. Around me the irises rustled their papery leaves. They unfurled their tongues, splayed wide their gullets and yawned down to the stamen, only to curve away, sting-like, in whorls of mottled flesh. They bore more resemblance to insects than plants, their palette of dark chocolate sigils a scribbled death's head – and they were already dying when I found them, dry blades clustered behind each fluted head.

The irises nodded and pointed. Upstream, the flowers said.

'Stay,' I said to Elijah, and he sat with a thump on my dungarees, his head on his paws, eyes accusatory. He whined as I swam off, a whine more like a chattering that resolved itself into a groan.

I followed the flowers into the fields, further than I

had ever been before, and where a plashing stream joined the river, I hung, while the current pummelled me. It was strange, treading the water, which seemed to be treading me back. After a while my body ceased to belong to me and the relief was intense. I could feel and not feel – or, rather, feel everything: the light, the branches, the water. I was wiped out, effaced, displaced, no thing in particular: a place, a process, a space through which other things passed. I was water, I was light; I was surely evaporating. For the space of a few seconds I was complete. It was what I had hoped God would do – was this God now?

I was trying to think, to ask myself what was happening, but something unearthly was building – I was stretched taut, my heart thundered, light burnt me up – and then right at the summit all things subsided into absence, or presence, I wasn't sure which – and even as I thought this I ceased to be aware of the thought and was aware only of stillness, the movement of trees, the bank bobbing, the water kneading me with its feet.

Then bank, trees and water all went crashing away as wave after wave of something else washed over me. I buckled, gasped, went under and came up, then clung to the bank as darkness swallowed me up.

When I opened my eyes I did not know how much time had passed. The sun was low and a breeze was stirring the irises, which made a sound like pages turning. It was a moment before I saw the eyes watching me, two slits in a head that sheered away abruptly. I jumped backwards, splashing, and the eyes slid away, and after them a long body, appearing first to the right of me, then to the left.

I dragged myself out, shaking, my limbs leaden and slow. I ran back along the bank. Elijah saw me from a distance and ran up, whining and yapping. My teeth were chattering so badly now that my jaw ached, and if I had wanted to shed my clothes before, I wanted nothing more than to put them on again, though I was clumsy and stumbled. Elijah kept glancing up at me anxiously, the little hairs above his eyes pointing this way and that. I did not pet him. All I wanted to do was get away from there. As soon as I had pulled on my clothes I began to run.

The light was different now, no longer white but golden and low. Sand martins were swooping, bobbing gnats auriferous specks in the air. We came up through the field, a stitch in my side and a heat low down in my body where God had entered me. Because that is what must have happened. Surely. God had finally made Himself known to me. I had felt Him – irrefutably. For a moment, perhaps several, we had been One. It was the fulfilment of my only desire. Why then was I so uneasy?

We got to the gap in the hedge and squeezed through. As we ran back through the garden, the force of its gaze struck me more powerfully than ever before and the unease quickened into dread. I left Elijah gulping from the water-pump, his sides bellowing, and went into the kitchen. My mother was at the sink. She turned and stared at me.

'Sorry—' I said. 'I went out . . .'

Her eyes took in my hair. She said: 'You went in the river.' She seemed incredulous.

'I didn't mean to!' I said.

We looked at each other.

'You've been gone hours.'

'I'm sorry! I fell asleep; I think that's what happened.'

'You think that's what happened . . .?'

'I'm sorry,' I said. 'It won't happen again.'

We heard my father arrive. My mother turned back to the sink. She said: 'Go and dry your hair.'

*

'You've caught the sun,' my father said to me at dinner. My mother's face was empty. I couldn't eat and asked to be excused.

That evening I stayed outside till the air was thick and soft, and the light was fading like smoke through the apple trees. I sat in the long field with Elijah, gazing at nothing. He was anxious and quiet beside me but for some reason I did not want to touch him. My heart beat strangely and I throbbed in the new place, too, that till this afternoon I had not known existed. God, I said, is this You?

At about eight o'clock we began to walk back. As we passed the sheep-dip by the corner of the house I heard them.

'She needs company!' my mother was saying. 'She needs something to do!'

'You're supposed to be teaching her!' my father said.

'It's not enough!' I had never heard my mother speak so forcefully. 'She's growing up, she needs friends, people – a *life*!'

'Then we'll find a school if that's what you want!'

'It's not what *I* want!' she said. 'It's not what *I* want!'

I felt sick and leant against the wall. It was their first fight since we had come to the farm and it was about me. They went on, talking about responsibility, decisions, 'input', a word my mother seemed to like. At last I could not listen any more and went down to the kennel with Elijah.

When I went back to the house my father was gone and my mother was sitting at the table. She said nothing. I sat down opposite her.

After what seemed like forever, she said: 'D'you have any idea how dangerous what you did today was? If something had happened to you no one would have known.'

'I'm sorry,' I said.

Elijah looked at me from the doorway.

'Promise you won't do it again,' she said.

'I promise.'

'You just walked out!' She didn't seem to believe it; I could hardly believe it myself.

We were silent a moment. Then I said: 'There was a snake in the water. I didn't think snakes could swim.'

She did not seem to have heard what I said, and when I looked up her eyes were terrible.

'I didn't mean to . . .' I said, tears in my voice.

She got up and said: 'I'm going to bed.'

There was nothing for it but to follow her up.

It was still light outside my bedroom window. I undressed gingerly, my skin already red. The sheets hurt and I threw them off. I wondered if I should try to tell my mother what had happened, but did not know myself.

The sky became inky at last, but not black. The night that came was blue like the day and the land moved under the light. A breeze came in through the window.

'What happened?' I said, and did not know how to answer. Then I said: 'I found God.'

God had rewarded my persistence. I got up and knelt by the bed.

'Thank you for choosing me,' I said. I supposed my life was complete.

That night I dreamt of a green snake that wound in and out of milky flowers. The heat burnt again in that new place.

'God—' I cried, and woke; put my hand there, and touched it.

The Book in the Garden

According to my father, a law spanned all creation, from the baby in the womb to the earth and the planets, the interaction of forces both centripetal and centrifugal. The law was simple, though there were different ways of explaining it: 'You reap what you sow' was one; 'A life for a life' was another. My father said if a sin was committed, the universe would know, the earth would remember and the perpetrator would reap his rewards in due season. It was not possible, he said, for it to be any other way. Seeds fell to the ground, died and sprang to life again, flowers bloomed and withered, all things returned whence they had come from and began again. There were plants, he said, that, when opened, displayed the teeth of dead men. There were fields whose soil was red with blood; the sea returned its cargo sooner or later and so did the earth.

I wondered about the farmer who had lived at the farm before us; I had walked amongst the trees in the garden and tried to guess which one he had chosen. The action begged questions: if punishment was indicative of crime, what was his? More worryingly, had the score been settled or was there some deficit still awaiting payment?

I went down to the river once more that summer to make sure nothing had changed; however, some things already had. The heat had gone and the land was divesting itself of greenness; the sky was no longer blue but overlaid with a luminous film of copper, and the sun was a blind spot pulsing behind high banks of cloud. My body was different too. I had been ill for days after I came back from the river;

sick and shivery, my skin agony to touch. I lay draped in wet towels as it turned purple, then red, then peeled off. I had to cover myself if I went outside after that, and those parts that clothes did not cover, my mother did with copious amounts of sunscreen.

The evening Elijah and I went down to the river, two larks were rising from the grasses and the dusk was like smoke. I stood by the water and did not recognize it. It did not glitter any more, but was sullen. The irises were dead. I began to walk back but had not gone far when Elijah began to bark in the long grass at the water's edge. I parted it and saw a grating, clicking cluster of limbs as big as a football. There were pulsing throats, glistening arms and legs and heads, clinging one to another, eyes half closed and deathly. I stared, then I ran. I never went back.

Shortly after this the illustrated bible also underwent a transformation. For some reason a number of things happened to other relics from our former life at this time: a picture of a stag that we had had for as long as I could remember fell and pierced itself on the coal scuttle; a clock belonging to my grandfather stopped working and cost too much to be repaired; a spring popped from the seat of the ancient chaise longue one evening when we were in the sitting room, startling us as much as if an arm had appeared from a grave. But it was the bible that left behind the biggest hole.

We had moved the kitchen table beneath the apple trees that summer and my father read there each evening until it got dark. I had wondered what it must have been like for the bible to find itself in a real garden: for real seeds, real petals, real insects to be alighting on its pages; to discover that however brilliant its colours it could never compare to those that shifted and deepened, became warmer and colder, or changed altogether in the blink of an eye.

'Now after these things it came about that the true God put Abraham to the test,' read my father. 'Accordingly He said to him . . . "Take, please, your son, your only one, whom you so love, Isaac, and make a trip to the land of Mount Moriah and there offer him up . . ." So Abraham got up early in the morning and saddled his ass and took two of his attendants with him and Isaac his son . . .'

I think it was the first night we had had to light the oil lamp, or perhaps we had sat down a little later than usual, but for whatever reason this particular evening we could not see the words as clearly as we should have done.

'Finally they reached the place that the true God had designated to him,' my father read, 'and Abraham built an altar there and set the wood in order and bound Isaac his son. Then Abraham put out his hand and took the slaughtering knife to kill his son. But God's angel began calling to him out of the heavens and saying: "Abraham, Abraham! Do not put out your hand against the boy and do not do anything at all to him, for now I do know that you are God-fearing in that you have not withheld your son, your only one, from me." At that Abraham raised his eyes and looked and there was a ram caught by its horns in a thicket. So Abraham went and took the ram and offered it up in place of his son . . .'

The lamp cast an eerie light beneath the apple trees, whose shadows loomed monstrous overhead. Every so often a moth fell onto the table, reversed frantically, wings quivering, flipped over and died. I didn't like to jump too often. I thought surely my father would move us inside, but he kept reading. I glanced at my parents. My mother's face was closed up, the soft weight of her cheeks and downcast eyes making her look, as she often did when my father read the bible or spoke about religious matters, as if she was reverently asleep. His own face and neck were red from scrubbing.

I was sitting beside him, staring extra hard at the page because I did not want to witness the death throes of one more moth, when I thought I saw something on the paper itself, but so small I could not be sure whether I was imagining it. The entity I saw was no bigger than a seed and almost transparent. What was more, it was moving. Was it one of the particles I had seen before? I wondered. This time there was one, not many. I blinked but the speck didn't clear. Then I spotted another, rounding 'thicket' and passing through 'slaughtering'. I wondered whether my father had seen them. My mother was sitting too far away.

Suddenly, as if making up its mind about something, the first speck scurried to the edge of the page. I waited for it to drop over the side but before it did my father turned over.

'Oh!' I said.

My father looked at me. 'What?' he said.

'Nothing.'

On the next page there were three particles, each scurrying in different directions. This time I *had* to find out if I was imagining things. I said: 'There's something on the page.'

My father looked closely, frowned, then blew hard. The specks seemed to know what was coming; they froze, only to scurry twice as fast afterwards.

My father said: 'What the—'

'What is it?' My mother leant over.

My father swiped the page with his hand and the particles vanished, as if liquidized. I stared at him. He began to flick through the pages. There were one or more on virtually every page.

'What are they?' I said.

Over the coming days we found particles in all of our books.

On Saturday my father came back from the town. The specks had a name: 'book mites'. The bible would have to be destroyed. He said: 'They must have been in the books that were here.'

He was not himself for some days. He took the bible, along with our other books, to the bottom of the garden where he made a bonfire, but he could not bring himself to set light to it.

My father's hands were too big for the new bibles we bought and he turned the pages with vicious little flicks. My mother and I did not look up while he read; we turned the pages quietly and were extra attentive. But we could not make sacred that which felt secular. The words did not feel the same any more; they, like the land, had become alien to us.

At the bottom of the garden the book pile gathered fungi. Foxgloves took up residence there; nettles, dock leaves. One afternoon, when clouds were flying and the garden was full of breezes and watery rustlings, I rummaged with a stick until I found the big bible. Snails had made shining paths across the cover and woodlice fell from the spine. Instead of gold leaf there was a spattering of white spots at the edges, and the pages were, if possible, even more wrinkled.

My arms and legs felt so heavy that I sat down on the ground. After a moment, I tried to pull back the grease-proof page from the picture of the garden. It tore wetly. A curtain had been rent. The Most Holy was now Most Ordinary. Beneath the veil were no longer sword and tree, serpent and errant humans, but an old world slowly dissolving.

Mutiny

Today began as a particularly dreary one here at Lethem Park, the sun hidden behind banks of cloud, neither cold nor hot, dark nor light. Eugene wet himself; Pam ate clay and had to have her stomach pumped; Margaret taught me a new stitch; Robyn's parents arrived to take her out for the day; Alice made Mary cry: nothing out of the ordinary at all.

It only started to get interesting this evening in the dining room. I had been watching Brendan all day. He was pale, paler than usual, and sitting very still. When he came into the lounge I got up to go over to him but Margaret shook her head, she stopped Pam and Robyn going over too. I put my hand up to Brendan in our special greeting but he didn't see; though he never looks at anyone directly, today he didn't even seem conscious that I was there. It worried me, especially after what happened the other day. Brendan had *The Cosmological Principle* in front of him as usual but he wasn't reading. He sat like a stone. How much longer would it be before he began to adjust to the new medication Lucas had put him on?

It was at dinner that things kicked off. I should say that dinner was worse than usual – perhaps that was what did it. Carol's gift to us this evening was a tray of watery carrots and peas that tasted exactly the same as each other, lumpy mashed potato, cabbage the consistency of wet tissue paper, and something that resembled meat. The gravy was congealed, the carrots cold, the cabbage sat in pools of tepid water and tasted vaguely burnt. The mince consisted of gristle in tomato sauce. I hid a lot of it in my napkin.

The dining room was fuller than usual; I think that was the other factor. Lucas wants more than one ward to eat together – 'like a family', he said. I have 'enjoyed' (if I can use that word in conjunction with mealtimes at Lethem Park) the evening meal a lot less since. I am frightened of quite a few of the patients from the other wards: Ivan, for instance, once pressed his erection against me in the corridor; Kirsty the albino looks daggers with her unearthly eyes; and Jim – who does not frighten but revolts me – produces an inordinate amount of stringy phlegm that he coughs into his hand. But Brendan has been coping with the new meal arrangement less well than I. He finds all people extremely challenging, so to have been in a room with more than fifty must have been intolerable.

He was sitting across from me, spearing a pea, which, once captured, he gazed at in horror for some minutes, before swallowing it with an agonized expression. Sometimes Brendan sums up my feelings about Lethem Park (and, I am sure, many other patients') so eloquently that I can't help laughing; he will pull a face or make a noise or a gesture that speaks volumes about a situation that is inde-scribable – if only he was aware of it.

At the urging of Sue, Brendan reached for another pea, wincing as he did so. As he raised it to his mouth, our eyes met. Facial expressions worry Brendan, so I stopped smiling and raised my hand in our star-shaped greeting. Reassured by this, he acknowledged me with a series of rapid blinks before returning to the business of eating the pea. He was breathing heavily. His eyes were half closed and every so often he groaned.

Pete said: 'All right there, Brendan? Not feeling hungry? Why don't you try some of the carrots?'

I took another mouthful. Chewing was difficult: Pam

was eating her own snot; Robyn was crying and, in the process, divulging the contents of her mouth, which Sue had just succeeded in feeding her; and Jim had begun to hack. I could feel the nausea coming like rain clouds travelling fast. The fork got heavier and heavier. I began to sweat. I propped my head on my hand and set my jaw hard. The nausea got worse, and my muscles began to feel sick, as if I had a temperature. I swallowed another forkful just as Jim coughed up a particularly large entity. I was just about to ask to be excused when Brendan let out a loud groan and brought his right fist down on the table. We all looked at him.

He groaned again. The sound was like that of a cow: heavy, mindless, desolate. He brought his fist down on the table again, making the trays and cutlery jump.

'Brendan, stop that, there's a good boy,' said Sue.

She forked together some mince and presented it to him but he cuffed her hand away and the mince landed in Robyn's face. Robyn began to wail. A number of patients were now mumbling and moaning. Sue seized one of Brendan's arms and tried to reach the other. Brendan rolled his eyes, groaned again and brought his other fist down.

Pete said: 'Brendan! Stop that! Come on, eat up, your dinner's getting cold.'

Brendan's eyes continued to roll. He took his dinner tray, lifted it high and brought it down with a stupefying crash, so hard that the water slopped out of my beaker. I looked around for Margaret but she was on the next table with Mary and Alice and Miriam. Pete and another male nurse jumped up and wrested Brendan's dinner tray from him. He sat swaying for a moment, growling unintelligibly, then began to pound the table with his forehead, his body rocking back and forth to such an extent I thought he would topple back.

'*Stop it, Brendan!*' said Pete. '*That's enough!*'

Others had begun to bang the table too – bang and rattle and rock; holler and groan and wail. The din was over-whelming. My heart was beating hard. I sat, faint and shaking, and watched the nurses run up and down. Then, hardly aware of what I was doing, I began to bang too – and for the first time in an age I felt blood in my arms and my legs and my chest, air in my lungs, and either I could not hear other things or I was not aware of them except as one is aware of others in a throng, as part of oneself: one mouth, one fist, one song.

The din grew, fists, trays, beakers rained down. Brendan's face was flushed, his eyes half closed; there were beads of sweat on his forehead. He was rocking so wildly that Pete and the other male nurse struggled to catch hold of him. I saw Pete haul him up by the back of his jumper. The next moment Brendan's dinner tray was flying across the room, catching a female patient in the face. Pete and the nurse grabbed his arms but before they could get them behind his back Brendan had upturned the water jug, his beaker and his chair.

Others followed suit; soon the air was full of flying food, trays and one or two chairs. A glass of water and a portion of cabbage, potato and gravy landed in my lap, Mary got mince in her hair; the best moment of all was when Carol caught a tray of her own food in the face through the serving hatch. The men had by now secured Brendan's arms and were trying to get him away from the table, but Brendan arched backwards, his legs kicking wildly. More nurses arrived. The kitchen staff ran to help out.

The upshot of it all is that there were twelve patients removed from the dining room, one of them in a strait-jacket. It is not a pretty sight to see someone buckled into a straitjacket, but as Brendan was carried off I have never seen him looking happier – if you could call the manic, wide-eyed expression on his face 'happiness'. He struggled wildly, but the moment they won his eyes became glazed. A trail of saliva hung from his mouth, which gaped in the closest thing to a smile I have ever seen on Brendan's face; I would go so far as to say he looked almost beatific. And though he had technically lost the battle, he struck me just then, carried off between Pete and two other nurses, as a victor, as some sort of idol – a pop star crowd-surfing, some sort of war hero, a football legend; a god.

Even after our leader was captured it was some time before things quietened. I am sure the dining room has never seen the like.

We are presently rejoicing in our separate cells. I am still shaky and feel quite weak, yet I am exultant: a revolution has been born! We are buzzing, we are brimming, we are humming with life! None of us knew we had it in us – it is surprising what lurks only an inch or two beneath the surface calm. My only concern is whether Brendan will be all right. I have an urge to tap out a message of courage on the hot-water pipes in the hope that he will hear it. I also want to thank him because today, for the first time in years, I felt alive, and I feel part of this community as I have never done before – at one with every idiot, lunatic and basket case, who are now my brothers and sisters. How can that be after twenty-one years? But tonight I was not myself. In fact, I hardly know who I was.

I drift into sleep, thinking about Lucas and what he will do – because he will do something, I am sure. There hasn't been this sort of disturbance for years, and that it should happen on Lucas's watch, after his 'improvements', in spite of his new regime – indeed, because of it – will not go down well. His initiatives have failed; surely tonight was proof. The scoreboard in the lounge – how will the nurses fill it in now? They could give us black marks from here to eternity and it still wouldn't be enough. And if everyone is in the doghouse the system collapses anyway.

No, Lucas will not like this. Reprisals will follow. The reaping will be grim. In which case I suppose I should revel in the moment and give no thought, just yet, to what we have sown.

The Agenda

The windows here are too high to see out of. I often think, when the sky is white and leaden as it is today, that they resemble the great sleepless eyes of classical gods, inscrutable in their vacuous watchfulness. There is something about those windows that reminds me of Lucas.

Buoyed by the events in the dining room, I have decided that I will suggest again the need for some adjustment to my regime when I go along to the Platnauer Room: namely, that the exhaustion makes it impossible to get up at 8.30 a.m., that Graded Exercise only aggravates my pain and muscle weakness; that going to bed at 9 p.m. is pointless because I don't sleep but lie awake, jumping from sub- to semi-consciousness; that I can fill in CBT forms till I am blue in the face but the anxiety only gets worse. In order not to forget anything – because while I am with Lucas I find it hard to think – I make some brief notes so that I will present my case in the best way possible.

There is a change in the doctor today: he is cooler, there is no dazzling smile. He puts his head around the door and says: 'Can you wait a minute?'

'Yes,' I say, and wait on the chair in the corridor.

I wait over five minutes, then he puts his head out again and says: 'You can come in now.'

Inside there is no 'Hello, Madeline,' no 'Good to see you, Madeline!', no 'How are you, Madeline?' Instead he says: 'Take a seat.'

Interesting. The god's waters are ruffled. I think he looks

a little sallow, a little dark beneath the eyes. Has he not been topping up his tan at the salon? Is there trouble at home with the Colgate wife? Is one of the perfect offspring sick? Or is this subtle change to do with *us*, his precious charges; are our paths more closely linked than I suspected? Can he not change a human being's life irrevocably, and go home in his sports car to his jacuzzi bath, dinner and scotch, unscathed? Do we, on occasion, actually make him as miserable as he makes us? Are we perhaps threatening his hopes of the consummate performance, not behaving as decent lunatics should? Have there been comments, in-department asides? Have the staff expressed their reservations about his treatment of us?

It is the ideal time to press my advantage. I take a deep breath. 'I have a few questions, Dr Lucas.'

He says: 'Yes?' That is all. I could actually like this Lucas; this faded shadow of the man.

'Well,' I say, unprepared for such humanness, 'I'm concerned about my treatment. I don't think it's working, to put it bluntly – or, at least, working as – you may think; I don't mean the hypnotherapy, I mean the other things . . .'

'You think a lot, don't you, Madeline? You like to know exactly what's happening.'

'I do,' I say.

'But we have discussed your concerns before. I hardly think they will have changed much in two weeks. I'm quite willing to listen to them but let's do it later, shall we? Let's get on with our work. That's the important thing. We'll come back to them, all right?'

I do *not* like him. I can think of nothing to say, except 'Fine—' rather hotly.

And then I see he is flicking through photocopies he has made of my journal, and when I see this, I forget my questions anyway. 'When did you do that?' I say.

'The xeroxes? Oh, a long time ago,' he says. 'Now what are we to make of this?'

And he begins to read aloud.

29 August

Dear God,

I have made a discovery: I can make You come to me. You came to me in the river. You filled me with Your spirit and I was wiped out. Now I can make You come back.

I have not told anyone. I was going to tell my mother but I like it that it is a secret between You and me. Perhaps You wouldn't come any more if other people knew.

I was afraid the first time You entered me because it was so sweet. It is pain and ointment, and while it lasts I am not here and I am no one.

I was afraid to begin with but I'm not any more. I wish when You come You would stay longer. I wish You would stay for ever. But perhaps I couldn't live if You did. God, when You come it is so sweet! It is so sweet I think I am going to die of it.

'Very mysterious; you've marked the entry with a cross.'

'Have I?' I look steadily at my knees.

'Yes. Don't you remember what that was about?'

'No,' I say, and I hold his gaze, then look away towards the window. 'It's a long time ago, you know.' I too can be inscrutable.

He flicks through the rest. 'The crosses become more plentiful towards the end of the journal, then almost cease altogether in the last two months. What does that indicate?'

'Perhaps they were good days,' I say. I put on my most helpful face, and I am pleased with myself, because this is *my* agenda and it is called: 'Appearing to be Cooperative'.

'They must be epiphanic from the terms you use to describe this one.'

'Perhaps they were,' I say. 'Children get excited about all sorts of things.'

'Do you have these experiences of God any more?'

'No.'

'Just this one year at the farm?'

'Apparently.'

He flicks on. 'But the crosses seem to coincide with events taking a turn for the worse. In the next entry your father loses his job again; that wouldn't make sense, God appearing to you and then punishing you. Rather a confused deity, I think.' He raises a dark eyebrow.

I shrug and once more hold his gaze, and presently I see I have won because he sighs loudly, taps the photocopies and says: 'Are you reading this?'

'Yes,' I tell him.

'Good. Keep it up. I'll expect you to have read to the end of September by next Friday. Now, hop onto the couch.'

'I have some questions I want to ask—' I say.

'We have only an hour, Madeline. I really don't want to cut short our facilitated recall time. It's by far the most important part of your recovery. Let's address these questions next time, all right?'

'But—'

I stare at him. He looks at me enquiringly. And just like that, he has won once again, and I must submit.

Black

I settle myself by the window and take out the journal. It is best not to think about it. Just begin. After I have read my quota, after I have taken myself back, gone as deep as I am able, I will go into the lounge and drink a draught of institutionalized oblivion from the waters of Lethe. This place, at least, is good for something.

10 September

Dear God,

> *Something has happened. It doesn't make sense. I thought You were helping us. Tonight when he came home Dad said he had no more work. It was horrible at dinner and afterwards he said Elijah had to sleep in the kennel from now on. (I put extra dog food in his supper when they weren't looking.) The blackness is back. I'm sure of it. Dad is trying to hide it but I can tell.*

I close my eyes. I try to remember that evening but can see only parts and the parts that I see I may have imagined. I need help. I need someone to intercede. I ask the girl whose journal it is to come to me now and stand in my place, to go back and relay the narrative for me. As it was – as it still is, for her, at this moment; which is the same moment I occupy, I suppose, just a different version of it. There is no one else to ask.

'Help me,' I say, 'because what I am doing, I am doing for both of us.'

She is silent. I give up talking to her and go over and

over the words on the page, trying to feel my way back. I don't know how much time passes. I know I want more than anything to close the journal and sleep. But giving up is not an option. Nor is sleeping. Not any more. The way out is through.

At last, she comes. I feel a softening somewhere, a layer giving way. Fibres part, the fog thins, and finally I see clearly – too clearly – the kitchen, the woman, the man and the girl I find so hard to believe was once me, I once her.

My father came in. He said: 'No more work.' He filled the kettle and turned the tap off. 'There'll be more in a while.' He plugged the kettle in. His eyes were very bright and very black. I knew what it meant.

'Right,' he said. 'There's ground to be cleared,' and he went out.

My mother smiled. She said: 'Why don't you go and help him?'

'Don't worry,' I said. 'He'll get more work.'

She looked up from wiping the chopping board. 'I know he will, love.' She seemed surprised.

'Good. He always finds more work,' I said.

She rinsed the chopping board under the tap. I looked at her closely but her face was clear and she seemed to believe what she said. 'Go out and help him, he likes it when you offer.'

I looked carefully at her. The flesh above her eyes was tight. Her hair stuck out at odd angles. I leant against her and breathed in its smell. Then I held her arms to her sides and she laughed. 'I can't stir like this, and you know how your father hates lumps in his gravy!'

I took my arms away. 'It's not his gravy,' I said. 'It's our gravy. Why is everything *his*?'

As she strained the potatoes in the sink a cloud of steam rose, whitening the window as if a giant had breathed on it. It made me nervous, thinking of a giant, like the gods that had lived in this land before, the ones my father said were dead. What if our God was not strong enough to protect us from them?

'Mum, are you okay?' I said.

She turned. 'Yes, my love. Why shouldn't I be?' She smiled again, then went back to pouring the potato water and tripped over Elijah who was sniffing hopefully at the frying pan. She said: 'Take him outside, will you?'

I called Elijah and we went out. It was hot but there was no sun and the sky had clouded over. We went into the garden. I could hear him before I saw him. There was the silky splice of the spade in the earth, then a gravelly chink, as if the spade had struck china; then an angry metallic bang as the stone landed in the barrow. I felt the noise in my chest. It made me feel feverish and shaky. I began picking up the stones. I didn't want to say: 'Shall I help?'

He pretended not to notice. After a minute he said with a smile that looked tortured: 'Soon have this cleared.'

His face was red, his mouth a hole. When he pushed the spade into the earth he made a noise like a roar. I hated him when he was like that. I wished *I* could make noises; I wished he had to listen to *me*. So I shouted as I lobbed a stone into the barrow, and he stared at me and said: 'What are you shouting for?'

I shrugged but my heart was beating hard. 'You do,' I said.

I smiled quickly but he knew I did not mean the smile. His expression darkened. He bent back over the spade.

Elijah did not get scraps at dinner that night. He sat on his back legs, watching us, one ear up, one ear down, asking questions with his eyes.

'It won't hurt him, he's too fat anyway,' my father said.

'He's not fat!' I said. 'Since when has he been fat?'

'And I think it's about time,' he said loudly before I had finished speaking, 'that he started sleeping in the kennel. That's what it's there for!'

I stared at him. 'He always sleeps in the house,' I said. 'What's wrong with him sleeping here?'

He didn't answer, just carried on spearing his potatoes, then took a swig of tea. Mum didn't look up.

I took my dish to the sink because I couldn't bear to have Elijah gazing at me any more and because I couldn't bear to sit opposite my father, and because I was feeling hot and tight.

He said: 'Ah, excuse me, there are two more people still eating!' My mother flushed.

I sat back down. She asked if we wanted more.

'What do we want *more* for?' he said. 'Keep it for tomorrow! There's another meal there!'

But we always had second helpings if there was food left. I decided it must be because of there being no work. My mother said nervously: 'Yes, they were big portions,' and took the pan back to the stove. I caught his eye. He cleared his throat and began to whistle but it didn't fool me. The blackness was back. I knew it.

Elijah watched while we dried up and while we sat by the woodstove, still waiting for his scraps. Finally I couldn't bear it any longer.

'There's nothing *for* you!' I said. 'There're no scraps tonight!' and I ran up the stairs and along the landing to my room, but he came to the bottom and looked up.

At supper I added more dog food to the bread and mashed it well, as he liked it. I stood over him till he finished eating so they wouldn't find out, and I cried when I took him down to the kennel and locked him up.

Dear God,

   He is horrible to me. I hate to be near him. Mum says I have to do lessons in the morning but as soon as I have finished, Elijah and I run over the fields. Anywhere, as long as we are away from him. Anywhere, so long as we can be by ourselves.

I rest my head in my hands and press my thumbs to my ears and try to remember those early autumn mornings. I suddenly remember that when my mother and I did lessons at the kitchen table, we could hear tractors in the cornfield. The sound was lazy and curdled in the air. What else? I ask the girl. What else is there?

In the garden there were dry brown weeds, fat dandelions and pink feather grasses that I scattered over Elijah. There were swallows in the barn and blackberries in the hedges. The leaves were tinged with carmine and gold, and the fields were strewn with bales that looked as if a giant knife had carved them from butter.

   The words the grass spoke were jumbled, the ribbon had knotted, it was twisted and tied in great sheaves, already dead. There was quietness amongst the stubble. It was uncomfortable to sit on and ugly to look at. If the grasses had been blades, they had become needles, and try as I might I couldn't pass through their eyes.

   The kitchen smelt fusty. Flies buzzed above the oilcloth. The bin needed emptying but my mother hadn't noticed so I did it instead. She was marking my exercise books and wrote 'Excellent' in the margin or drew a star. Her stars were fat and looked happy, the points uneven, as if they were dancing on their toes or waving their fingers. Sometimes she drew a face on the star. When she was not marking she stared into the distance. When my father came in she went back to marking.

I was working out whether two thirds was equivalent to four sixths or ten fifteenths.

'Both,' a voice said.

He was looking over my shoulder. I flushed but didn't immediately write the answer. I pretended I was seeing whether what he said was right.

'How can you work like that?' he said as he went away. He meant work like that with Elijah's head on my lap.

I pushed Elijah away and bent over my book but my heart was beating too hard to think. I put my hands over my ears. He went to the sink to get a drink and my mother gestured for me to pass her my maths book. She made a flourish of ticking the page, then said loudly: 'Look at that: eight out of ten!'

I wondered how he could let me know just by the back of his head that he wasn't impressed. Was it to do with the way his neck was set, the strength in it, how it was somehow compressed? Was it the way his hair curled spitefully, as if it couldn't bear to be next to itself and hated the world? It was like a child's hair, the way the curls jostled. He carried on looking out at the fields where the tractor was. There was an oval of sweat on the back of his shirt. I put my sleeve to my nose.

23 September

Dear God,

Today he made Mum look like a fool and she didn't know what to do or say. There is no limit to my hatred for him.

I am with the girl again. We are in the garden. The air is full of heat and the smell of dung and hay. The grass is brassy against my legs. It is stiffer than it has been in the summer and rustles when the wind comes. The flowers look heavy, their heads fleshy and browning at the tips. The colours seem to have become even brighter, just before they must fade: the brambles blaze, the sky is bruised and damson, the roofs strawberry, the roses bloody or yolk-yellow. The world seems like a picture from a book from long ago, when the hues glow.

My father is still clearing the ground. The heap of stones is even bigger. He barrows them to the bottom of the garden then comes back for more.

'We'll be able to make a rockery soon,' my mother says.

'I don't know how they managed to grow anything here!' He stands up, straightening his back.

'Maybe it's just around the house,' she says.

'Don't be stupid – it's the same all over the island!'

I wonder whether this is true, whether the ground is stony everywhere. I wonder why he has to be unkind to her.

24 September

Dear God,

Today we helped him in the garden with the stones again. The stones were crawling with things and every time I touched one I wanted to retch.

I hated touching those stones. He says that gods lived here. Sometimes in the garden I think I can feel their bones beneath the grass and hear their voices in the trees. The stones are their eyes – or perhaps they are their hearts. We should leave them where we found them, in the dirt and the dark.

We were at the table when my father came in. He said: 'Give me a hand, will you?' His face was dark red. He was angry at having to ask for our help and angry at us for being there to ask, but it wasn't a question anyway. We closed the books and went out.

My mother had the spade with the broken handle and she had to keep stopping to tape it up. Her body juddered as she dug because she was digging so hard. Her hair was slicked over, her mouth open. She grinned and said: 'All right, love?' Why does she always look so silly? Are some people just like that?

When I threw the stones into the barrow Elijah yapped and jumped at them. He knew they were only old stones but he was bored and trying to amuse himself, he was very clever like that, he could pretend the same as I could. I think he was also trying to cheer me up, cheer us all up, but it didn't work.

'Take that dog away from here!' he said.

I hated doing it. I took Elijah up to the courtyard and told him to stay in the house. He put his head on his paws.

'It's all right,' I said. I cupped his nose in my hand. 'You haven't done anything wrong. He's just grumpy.'

He wasn't any happier with Elijah gone. We worked all afternoon but the stones kept appearing. They were crawling and slithering with things. They were pale and round, almost circular. I thought they looked like the eyes of statues. Once I thought that, I didn't want to touch them any more, or see them in the pile, or watch them fall thundering onto the grass.

The next day I didn't want to be where my father was so I sat with Elijah in the kennel. He was chewing a piece of wood, snuffling and sneezing when bits got up his nose.

'Do you understand what's happening?' I said.

He snuffled and shook his head to clear his nostrils.

'Neither do I,' I said. 'I wish God would talk to me. I want to ask Him questions.'

I stroked Elijah and watched tractors in the long field.

The engines rippled through the afternoon like slow farts. The sound came towards us, then faded again on the thin breeze. The great arms lifted the bales into the air so that they sailed for a little while in the white sky. Everything seemed pointless. I lay back in the straw and made God come to me. There was still that.

The sky was white. I didn't know where the blue had gone. Every day the land lost a little more colour. The orchard smelt of cider and water and old leaves. The ground was soggy and the air filled with wasps and flies. One afternoon my mother and I held bedsheets under the apple trees while he climbed up and shook them.

The apples were foamy, the flesh fibrous, the skins loose. We washed them and laid them on newspaper in the chests upstairs in the dairy. My father said we had to collect more.

'Leave spaces!' he said. 'Or they'll go bad.'

He snatched an apple out of my mother's hand and relaid it, and she seemed to shrink as if she were plastic and a flame had been held up to her. I glared at him; I didn't care if he saw that I hated him.

'What?' he said.

'Nothing.'

My temples hurt. I went into the yard and swung the rope with the stick at the end for Elijah. I swung it so fast you could hear it slicing the air. I swung it till my shoulder was burning, then swung it some more.

I decided not to call him 'Dad' any more; he was not my father and never had been.

I get up from the chair and move to the bed. I curl on my side and begin reading the journal again, where I left off.

27 September

Dear God,

Where do You take me when You come? Today I made You come to me in bed and everything went away. But afterwards I felt empty and the world was dark. When I am sad the world seems darker still. Can that be true? I have noticed something else too: when I am sad the ground seems close, as if I am going to bump into it. It has been feeling close for over a week now.

I can't go out to the fields because it is wet. Besides, I have found You, there is no point in looking for You any more.

29 September

Dear God,

The world still seems dark today, as if it has been unplugged. In the afternoons after Mum and I have finished lessons I go down to the stream. In the stream there are small animals. I call them crayfish. Mum doesn't know what they are either. They are like small grey shrimps. There are pools in the stream, dams and waterfalls I have made, marked with stones. They smell of ponds and mud and saliva. Clouds and shadows move upside down in them. Beside the largest pool is a stone. It is made of the same stone as the millstone beside the front door, and when the sun catches it, it flashes colour like a diamond.

I was patching a leak in the dam of the top pool when I saw one crayfish carrying another. I've never seen that before. The one underneath was hollow and looked white. I wondered whether they were eating each other. The more I watched the surer I became. I fished them out and separated them on the rock but couldn't be sure whether I was hurting them as I had to pull them apart. I put the white one back in the water and he sank, then puttered along the bottom.

I was shaking. It made me sick having to touch them even though I was using a stick. I didn't know what to do with the other one. Why should he go back into the water just to eat someone else? He was walking on his side on the rock, making his way back to the water. I took my knife and crushed him with the side of it. I did it quickly and pressed very hard because I was frightened. I pressed so hard there was immediately nothing but grey juice.

I sat back and suddenly felt dizzy. I wiped my hands on my jeans, though nothing was on them, and I had to get up and walk around before I could go back to the stream. For a minute, after I had cried, the day got brighter again, as if someone had plugged it back in.

I washed the rock and wiped the knife clean. I looked for the hollow crayfish but couldn't find him.

I am going to go down to the stream tomorrow, and if I can, I will save another life.

I remember that clearly, every detail. I turn over and lie on my back because my heart is beating hard, because I am torn between reading on and getting this over with, between stopping here and putting it off.

1 October

Dear God,

We have spaced the apples like he said but the badness seems to travel anyway. Today when Mum and I went upstairs in the dairy we found sagging patches of scented brown flesh. Mum said: 'It must be the weather.' She looked frightened. She said: 'We'll get rid of them.'

We took the apples and hurled them over the fence at the bottom of the garden. I had to stop Elijah bringing them back. Then we rearranged the others and put them in the places where the bad ones had been. We went inside with more apples in our jumpers and she set me lessons. When I had finished I helped her. All afternoon we peeled and cored and baked and stewed and fried apples. Then we began on the potatoes.

'The nights are drawing in,' he said, coming in from clearing brambles. He was soaked through. I didn't think we needed to clear any more but he is always doing something even if there is no point to it. He didn't have to say that, either: 'The nights are drawing in' – it made my stomach turn, it made me frightened for nothing.

'Fantastic!' he said at dinner. 'Food from our own garden!' But he was just pretending to be jolly. The blackness is there, I know. I'm watching him. It came out when I said I was full and couldn't eat any more. 'We don't have any waste in this house!' he said. So I wasn't allowed to leave any of my stewed apples – though usually he is telling us to keep leftovers for tomorrow. He makes up his own rules.

If I never see another apple in my life it will be too soon.

3 October

Dear God,

The blue has finally come back. When I get up the sunlight is like a needle over the rim of the hills and there is a mist of water at the corners of the window-panes. The air feels clean. Breezes have taken away the smell in the kitchen.

We went preaching today with apples and potatoes in our lunchboxes. We ate lunch in a lane. The man who is technically my father thanked You for giving us the apples and potatoes. I wondered whether I should say 'Amen' because I would be lying. He made noises when he ate, smacking his lips, and I hated him. There was a little bit of ham, which I saved for last, to take away the taste of the apples and potatoes. We didn't get to share any verses from the bible except with an old lady who we thought might have been deaf.

This afternoon I asked Mum when we would run out of apples and she said she thought there were enough to last all winter. I went up to the dairy and took an armful of apples and moved the others around to fill up the space. I put the apples in my pockets and went down the lane with Elijah. When we were a few fields away I threw them as hard as I could against a tree. Pieces of apple brain splattered against the bark. I went back to the dairy and did the same all over again. It felt good. It is a sin to hate my father but not to throw apples.

6 October

Dear God,

I made You come to me three times this morning. I wonder if You come to other people in the same way. I thought again about telling Mum. I don't know why I didn't. Anyway, she wouldn't believe me. No one would. But I know it's real. I suppose I wouldn't know if other people had found You or not. I still think I am probably the only one.

We ate apples for breakfast, lunch and tea. I asked Mum whether they were the fruit Adam and Eve ate in the garden. She said she didn't know but it was probably something more exotic. I said I thought it must be because no one could be tempted by an apple.

7 October

Dear God,

There is something wrong with Mum. Today while we were doing lessons she kept rubbing her eyebrow, running *her finger over it again and again. Every time she looked at me she smiled. I wished she didn't think she had to do that.*

When I gave Elijah his dinner the man who is married to my mother told me to mix bread with the dog food. 'And don't give him any more,' he said. Elijah looked at his bowl and then at me. I don't blame him. 'At least you don't have to eat apples,' I said. 'Think about that.'

In the afternoon we went preaching on the bikes. I felt sick as we rode down the drive and I felt sick when we walked down the tracks and knocked on the doors. It was farms mostly and the people didn't want to know. It was hard concentrating at all in the end. The sickness was so bad I began to sweat. It got harder and harder to pedal. I had to tell them and we came back home. Mum pushed my bike for me and Dad pushed both of theirs.

'We'll soon have you right,' she said.

But at home after she had given me Gaviscon she fell asleep at the table. Her face was grey and a little pool of spit formed under her mouth. Her eyebrows were raised as if they were clinging to something and her breath made the pocking sound. We used to find her asleep like that when we lived in the town.

At dinnertime he clattered saucepans but she didn't wake. His eyes were hard and flashing. I thought she looked frightened. I helped him wash up, then Elijah and I went down to the stream. I found three crayfish eating others and killed them on the rock with the knife that has the red cross on it. I put the victims back into the pool but I think I was too late and one was already dead.

There was no point washing the rock because there will soon be more blood on it. I called Elijah and we came back up to the house. It was dark and she was still sleeping.

I just heard a scream outside. It is five past eleven. I've heard the noise before. Mum said it was a rabbit. The noise sounds like flesh and blood. It is terrible. When I asked what was happening to the rabbit, she wouldn't tell me.

God, please don't let her get ill again.

10 October

Dear God,

Today we had our first frost. It rose from the ground and stayed all day and it was so quiet I could hear the hooves of the horses trampling the stubble in the field.

This evening we went to the supermarket. Elijah sat by the door, whining to be allowed to go with us. It has been harder to leave him lately. 'We'll be back before you know it,' I said. 'Really.' Mum and I sang on the way to town. The man who lives with us heard about some work in the supermarket. I hope he gets it, and stays out of the house.

He was all right again when we got home, lighting the fire, drinking his lager in the long, smooth, slow way he does. Mum looked happy. I went outside with Elijah and the moon was huge. I ran around the courtyard and it was as if I was saying something, only not out loud. Writing words on the night.

My father's fist was red on the gearstick, which stuck and grated. His arm was resting on the window and the breeze came in sharp and chill. The frost had disappeared and the air was bitten and I could smell the land as if it had just been made; I could smell wild garlic in the hedges, and the earth, and the reek of silage and, once, the sharp tang of fox. 'The nights are drawing in,' he said. I looked at the river and saw he was right; the light was tired, and something tugged at the pit of my stomach.

My mother sang 'Three Wheels on my Wagon' on the way into town in the car. She was cold and stiff but singing away, wearing lipstick and her favourite pink jumper beneath her coat. She had cut her fringe and it was skew-whiff but she didn't seem to notice. The jolts of the car were making her voice shake, making it sound silly. I thought he might be driving extra fast on purpose, so I joined in.

We were getting a trolley by the door of the supermarket when a man in overalls and builder's boots passed by. My father said: 'Excuse me, d'you know if there's any building work around here?'

'Masses of it down by the river,' the man said. 'They're building a new cinema. Go and put your name down, they can't get enough men.'

While my mother and I got groceries he went to find the site. We were at the checkout when I heard a slap and my mother jumped. My father said: 'What's the little woman got for me, then?' He was holding an off-licence bag and he looked triumphant.

My mother flushed. 'Did you get it? Did you put your name down?' She looked like a little girl.

'Aye, aye,' he said, frowning now slightly, as if it was suddenly unimportant, because she had asked, all eager like that. He began swinging bags of shopping into the trolley.

On the way home my mother was loose and warm beside me. We sang 'Three Wheels on my Wagon' again but this time it was easy, our voices were louder and we were laughing. My father beeped in time. 'God provides!' he said. But he hadn't been so sure earlier.

I was allowed to give Elijah dog food without bread that night. They lit the woodstove. It was the first evening they had lit it. He turned off the light and opened the door and it made shadows in the room. He drank lager and gave my mother a wineglass full of it. I sat on the orange and brown carpet, and Elijah lay with his head in my lap, and for an hour or two everything was all right. My mother fell asleep at last but her face was rosy and looked peaceful, not dead and white. Sitting there with the flames flickering, I suddenly felt unusual, sort of powerful, and I had to go out.

In the courtyard bats were fluttering, the moon sailing. Blackness washed around us like water. There was white light and yellow light: white from the moon and yellow from the lantern high on the end wall of the house. Beyond the circle of light there was darkness; shed doorways gaped, fields were eaten up. I stood in the centre and raised the rope above my head.

Elijah's ears pricked up. He yapped sharply and bounced on his front paws. The rope sliced through the light, a dark line flashing over cobbles and walls, vanishing and re-appearing, and his shadow leapt with it, writhing, twisting, up, up, up higher, like a fish on a line, hanging upon nothing, as God hung the earth, with only space all around, then dropped back to rejoin him, skittering stones.

The rope spun past the numbers at our feet. I banished them to infinity. There was fire in me; I was writing a word, tracing dark letters on the light. I began to run, the rope whizzing, up the steps in the wall by the sheep-dip, along the top, across the roof of the barn and down the stones in the corner. I ran up the plank at the other side, onto the garden table, along the wall, jumping from pillar to pillar, and as I went – wherever I went – I took the light with me.

Elijah chattered and yelped. I circled faster and beneath me my shadow hurdled the world. My steps rang over the land and returned to me from the eye of moon.

'D'you see that?' I shouted. 'Do you see what I can do?'

The blackness seethed and shivered, it tossed and it muttered, but it couldn't enter the circle because I was guarding it.

The Cost of Memory

In the Platnauer Room I see many things. I see the frost on the gatepost at the farm, which came in the mornings and disappeared, leaving the shape of my hand. I see the forests of lichen on the apple-tree boughs that seem like something from the ocean floor. I see the way the mist lifts from the fields so that the world is full of the top halves of things. I see the way the sun breaks through the clouds and turns the world white with vapour as veil after veil of spirits rise. I see the little weed balls that catch in Elijah's haunches and groin and his sweet underbelly where the domed ribs rise warm beneath my hand like the timbers of a living cathedral. I see a line of geese in the cold blue dawn wipe the eye clean and make the mind dumb.

I have gone back many times now. The light moves, the numbers descend, I slip lower. With each word I go back, I go deeper, I go down, unwinding the thread along the dark passage, gathering sticks on the floor of my mind, laying a trail for the one who comes after. The doctor treads heavily, he follows me hither and thither, getting hotter and more bothered; he does not let me stray far. I am a good animal most of the time. I walk at his pace, not pulling, not lagging, not darting away to sniff this or that. But just sometimes I think I might slip out of my leash and into the dark, and watch him continue – readily for a while, then more slowly, groping, stumbling, getting up again; calling my name; asking me where, asking me when, asking me why.

Yet the key things, I do not remember. But it is not just

I who have the monopoly on amnesia: forgetting is the precondition of existence; we forget to stay alive, filter the necessary from the unnecessary, the bearable from that which can't be borne; whether or not we are aware of it, we leave what we have to the dark. Memory perpetuates pain and forgetting removes it – at least consciously. Lucas believes that if truth is thwarted one way, it will find another way out. I think he too has difficulty remembering, or at least remembering that which he chooses to ignore.

There has been no mention, by Lucas or any of the other staff, of the events in the dining room. In this case the 'least said, soonest mended' philosophy seems to have been adopted; I wonder whether it was a new initiative. There have, however, been reprisals. Lucas has revoked his decree that we eat en masse and now when our ward eats, we are by ourselves as we used to be in the small room adjoining the lounge. Moreover, owing to the fact that everyone has accrued so many black marks for their involvement in the fracas, the scoreboard in the lounge has been wiped clean and we all have a new start. That includes even Brendan. Though we haven't seen him since.

'Where's Brendan?' I asked Margaret yesterday. Her cheeks were red and she had a scratch above her right eye.

'In his room with Pete,' she said.

'What's Lucas done to him?' I said.

'Nothing,' she said, 'he's just taking things quietly.'

I asked her if I could go and see him but she said he would be sleeping and I could do it tomorrow. No one else seems to miss Brendan. They have forgotten their leader entirely, though the effects of his uprising are still being felt: Miriam has been singing hosannas, Pam and Robyn painted a picture together, and altogether the ward has been more peaceful. It is nothing short of miraculous, what our little demonstration has accomplished! A little rebellion goes a long way here, and this one will sustain us, I should think, for quite a while.

As for me personally, I do not seem to be doing so well.

'You're resisting, Madeline,' Lucas tells me as I come round today. 'I need you to understand that the work we're doing is of the greatest benefit to you, though it may feel difficult.'

'I'm sorry,' I say. 'If I am resisting, I'm not aware of it.'

Lucas is frowning, looking at me with the air of an army officer reassessing the defences of a fortified city; apparently I am not proving to be the easy conquest he thought. I have reserves he knew nothing of.

'Whenever we get close to the night you ran away your subconscious veers off,' he says.

He closes his eyes a moment and rubs the bridge of his nose. I consider raising my questions again, regarding the efficacy of the regime. I even consider asking how Brendan is. But Lucas is playing his part – the caring therapist – and I must play mine. I must not arouse suspicion because Lucas has an agenda and I am part of it: he stands to win or to lose depending on the result of my treatment. His agenda is called: 'An Experiment in Amnesia Disguised as Helping a Patient'. My case, like Job's, has interest merely for the amount of light it can shed on issues of sovereignty – for what are men such as Lucas but pastors of the mind, and as such the guardians of humanity? And what better than to allow the omnipotent one to believe I am a malleable idiot ignorant of his personal point scoring?

In any case, I have an agenda too, entitled: 'Release'. Everyone has an agenda, it's just a question of who reads whose first. If, however, I am to be a pawn deployed to prove or disprove some point of theory – which will, when it is masterfully researched and illustrated, be filed away on a shelf somewhere – then it is crucial to let the mover believe the pawn *is* a pawn and oblivious to his intent.

'I know you have my best interests at heart, Dr Lucas,' I say. I feel a pain in my temples as I do so, somewhere between an itch and the feeling I used to get when I travelled in cars, a sort of toxic fatigue akin to nausea.

'Good,' he says. 'It's important that you know it's perfectly safe to access information here because this is where it can be dealt with. In the wrong environment it would be disastrous.'

The worst of it is that Lucas could simply be one more projector; I do not know whether what he shows me is truth or my own imaginings. He wants to resuscitate me, reintroduce me to what I once was. Or does he? Is this another shadow, a smokescreen for more private interests, and do the waters he wakes me from part only to reveal another, deeper slumber, more profound than any I have previously known? Is it wiser to dream along with him in this sleep of the soul than to wake to one more profound? Must I go deeper to get out? And do not think I have not asked myself what would happen if I were to wake and find beyond the visible, on the inside of this husk, no meaning at all.

'I understand,' I say. I am beginning to sweat.

'But your subconscious doesn't. Not yet.' He looks at me: 'Madeline, I need you to bear in mind that if things go on like this we may have to resort to pharmacologically facilitated interviews.'

'What?' I say.

'Drugs will make it easier, for you and for me.'

I should have expected treachery. 'I don't need drugs!' I say.

He crosses the room and settles all six foot six of him in the black leather chair, crossing his long legs, the brogues glinting malignantly. Upside down in them I can see the whole room, right down to my white face peering back; even in the brogues I look stricken.

'Well,' he says virtuously, 'for the time being we'll perse-
vere. I sometimes liken this sort of work to felling a tree:
nothing seems to be happening – then suddenly – timber!
– and the whole thing comes crashing down.'

I close my eyes.

'Where have you got to in the journal?'

'October.'

'You have to read more, all right?'

'All right.'

He frowns again. 'You ran away,' he says. 'You were an
obedient child, you were uneasy when you were absent
from the farm, and yet you ran away. What caused you to
do something so uncharacteristic?'

After some time I open my eyes: 'I was upset, I suppose.'

'Well, obviously. But why run away? I understand the
crisis with your mother – but you were so close to her, so
why didn't you want to stay? Why run away, Madeline?
Why run away?'

I look away. 'Does everything have to have a logical reason?
I was upset . . . I don't know . . . It was so long ago!'

As I speak, I sense something behind me and the sensation is so strong that for several seconds I do not turn my
head.

Then he says: 'Madeline—' and when I do turn to look
at him I jump violently. He is leaning forwards, almost
touching the hem of my skirt, and his voice, while still
excited, is different; fervent and low. He says, smiling gently,
in a soft voice: 'What if I told you I don't think you're the
quiet girl everyone believes you to be?' Then, in an even
softer voice: 'That I don't think you've forgotten anything
at all?'

I see his lips form the words, I hear them, but I cannot
be sure whether he spoke or I only imagined it, and for a
moment – the kind that happens in our worst nightmares,
in which what we have been ignoring turns, by some

lightning stroke, into the very apotheosis of horror; or, worse, in some essential way into ourselves – I am sure that I have always known him; he is the fear in the dark, the creature in the corner, the depthlessness of great distances, the eyes in the garden, the voice of the river, the figure in clouds, the blood on the stone. But what does he *want* from me? *What has he always wanted?*

As if a switch has been flicked we are back. I can hear our breath and the ticking of the heating in the pipes and a door closing somewhere along the corridor and distant voices, all reassuring in their familiarity, yet at this moment nothing but sounds on a pre-recorded reel. I can see the lamp and the iPad, the desk and his chair, but they are no more than shapes on a screen – and even Lucas, for one dazzling moment, is also something I have constructed, or am reflecting: me and not me. I am not his patient, he is not my psychiatrist. We are not sitting in a lamp-lit room in an asylum for the mentally insane in the heart of the English countryside; we are antagonists locked in an age-old struggle, shadows in a show played out across the cosmos, before an invisible audience, at no particular time and in no discernible place, to prove or disprove a point of eternal doubt.

I sit back and so does the doctor, who seems to be taking his cue from me. I am winded; he blinks as if waking, collects himself, frowns and begins to shuffle papers. He does not appear to know any more than I do what just happened.

'Keep reading the journal,' he says brusquely. 'That's the most important thing for now.'

The Idea

The girl leads the way, I follow. She is always near now; to slip inside her as easy as slipping into a fast-running stream. I do not have to court or to coax; sometimes it is I who ask to stop and wade back towards the bank, where I sit shivering.

'I don't understand,' my mother said quietly.

She was blinking. We were sitting in the car in the supermarket car park. She was afraid and I felt sick because I could see how hard she was trying not to show it.

'Neither do I!' he said. 'All I know is I've just been down to the building site and there isn't any.'

My mother's eyebrows went up and she smiled uncertainly. 'But you put your name down . . .'

'I *know*!' He passed his hands over his hair, stared ahead for a minute, then got out and slammed the door. We followed him into the supermarket.

He took a basket and gave it to my mother, who hurried after him.

I said: 'Can I wait here?'

'All right,' he said. 'Stay on that seat by the door.'

On the seats I leant my head on my hands and tried to think clearly. The people on the island didn't like my father because he was different to them; there *was* work but he wouldn't get it. If God wanted to help us He could. So we must have displeased Him; we must have broken the covenant, been disobedient in some way. I just didn't know how.

When I opened my eyes two girls were staring at me. My stomach flipped over. I tried to think what I had been doing; I had been passing my hands back and forth over my head. I put my hands in my lap. One girl whispered to the other and they walked away, laughing at me.

I pulled my jacket down over my dungarees. I noticed for the first time that the cuffs ended above my trainers; I saw that my socks showed. A voice made me turn.

He was at the checkpoint, saying: 'How can it be that much? It's on special offer!'

'No,' said the cashier. 'Not these; the ones next to them.'

My mother was smiling but the smile was fixed, as if she wasn't actually smiling at anything in particular.

'Well, take them off, then!' He was red in the face. 'I don't want them at that price! It's daylight robbery!'

The bags of shopping sat heavily beside our feet on the way home. The evening air came in through the window, smelling of silage and cold. Suddenly the fields and the emptiness and the road stretching out endlessly in front of us made me want to run.

His face was set like stone but his body seemed to be pulsing. My mother touched her cheek. She put out her hand to hold on to the dashboard when we hit a pothole. I was glad I was sitting next to him, between the two of them. She was like a bird, trembling. When I looked at her I felt a pulling in my stomach and I wanted to touch her. He was pulsing with rage beside me but when I looked at him the pulling in my stomach was even stronger and I didn't know why.

When we next went into town we saw some builders. My father stopped the car. 'Any work, boys?' he said.

'What was that?' one shouted back.

'Any work?'

'Not that I know of,' the man said. He had hair as black

as coal and pale blue eyes. He reminded me of a wolf. He gazed at my father and then at the car.

My father said: 'There seems to be quite a bit of work here.'

The man laughed, a light blow-away sound. 'Ah, you'd think so, wouldn't you? But we're just about full here.'

My father laughed then. 'There's— six of you,' he said, 'and there's a lot of blocks there, boys.'

'So there are,' said the man. The blue eyes barely blinked.

'Right,' my father said. 'Well. Just thought I'd ask.'

'Aye. No harm in asking,' said the man.

My father started the car but the engine stalled. He started it and it stalled again. He started it and it stalled once more. He started it again and gunned it hard, and we drove away with a ripping sound of tyres on tarmac. When I looked back at the man he was smiling and so was another.

My father whistled through his teeth on the way home. He swerved to miss all the potholes. A car overtook us just before we turned off the main road, flashing its lights. 'POLICE', it said on the side. The exhaust wasn't rattling, so I guessed it could have been about there being no seatbelt.

My father didn't say anything but his eyes were glinting and I knew he was afraid. One of the officers got out of the car and walked towards us. When he got up close he peered at us, then looked back into the car and said to my father: 'You know it's illegal to drive without your tax disc on display?'

My father said he did but he was waiting to register the car and for that he needed the car to be weighed and other information to fill in the form. And he was – he'd been waiting weeks for a letter giving him an appointment to have the car weighed but it hadn't come. The man glanced up the road and then back at him.

'I'll give you five days to get it sorted,' he said. Then he turned and walked away.

My father sat staring at the steering wheel for a minute, then got out and slammed the car door shut. He called the policeman. Through the back window my mother and I saw them speaking. The policeman shook his head and flicked his fingers. He carried on walking back to his car and got out some papers. He nodded once in the direction of the town, his expression dangerous, on the edge of something, then got into his car and drove off.

My father got back into our car. He said: 'This country is run by lunatics!'

My mother said: 'I don't know what he's on about – you can't get the car weighed before it's taxed, and you can't get it taxed before it's weighed. They must know that.'

My father started up the engine again and he had the sort of stillness about him he got sometimes, as if something were gripping him. He was sitting slightly skew-whiff in the seat. I didn't have to look at his face to tell how he was feeling – each of his hands was angry; the little gold hairs jutted out from the backs of his fingers and his knuckles were white on the wheel. My mother was looking straight ahead, the skin tight over her eyes, her eyebrows raised in tiny triangles. Her mouth and nose were pink and almost quivering. After that I didn't look at either of them but straight ahead at the road, which twisted between hummocks of gorse and hills and fields and brown-and-cream bungalows.

When we got home she had fallen asleep and he took tea out to her. I decided to call him 'Dad' again.

25 October

Dear God,

It seems that everything Dad liked about this place in the beginning he hates now. The roads aren't 'fantastic', they're riddled with potholes; people don't 'give it to you straight', they haven't got any manners; this isn't our long-lost home but a holiday gone sour. That's what he said today: 'It's like a holiday gone sour.'

So what does this mean? It means You — or we — have broken the covenant. Which is it? How? And why?

Mum didn't take her coat off today. It's hard for her to stay awake in the cold. We didn't do lessons because she hadn't prepared any. She didn't do anything but sit with a cup of tea, her hand around the handle, gazing at nothing.

I read the bible in my room, killed more crayfish in the stream and made You come to me because I was bored.

26 October

Dear God,

This evening we read about Abraham and Isaac again. Afterwards Dad prayed and said that he had faith and asked for forgiveness and to be directed to work. He said he knew that this was a test, and we would come through it. For a minute, after he had finished praying, he looked peaceful. Then Mum asked whether she could light the woodstove and his face clouded.

The first match went out. She struck another and it happened again. He stared at her; she was blinking. He stood behind her and she struck a third and her hand was shaking and the match died. Then something snapped in him and he yelled: 'What's the matter with you?'

She bowed her head. He snatched the matches from her, his eyes flickering, struck one and it flared first time.

'Are you all right?' he said, and it was as if he had barked at her. His eyes bored into her, and then just when I didn't think I could bear him looking at her like that any longer he took a bottle of White Lightning into the study.

My heart was beating so hard it was making me feel faint. I didn't go to her because I knew she didn't want me to have seen, so I went outside. Elijah was lying in the courtyard, chewing his stick. He jumped up when he saw me and we walked to the gate. I climbed over, he slipped through, and we kept on going.

I didn't know where we were heading. I couldn't see because I was crying. Elijah glanced at me anxiously every now and then. He butted my hand and pressed against me, and I curled my hand along the side of his nose and held him there.

27 October

Dear God,

Today I thought about Abraham going up to the mountain with Isaac again. I know that Abraham had great faith and didn't really have to kill Isaac, and I know that the story foreshadowed You and Christ, who really was sacrificed, and wasn't saved at the last moment by a ram. And I know You are allowed to test us whenever You like. But was it right, God, to test Abraham like that?

1 November

Dear God,

He has gone into the junkyard in town with things to sell. I am sitting at the kitchen table doing sums and Mum is sitting by the grill. We have our coats on. There is not enough wood to light the woodstove and coal is too expensive. We are allowed the grill on number one but Mum has it on number two. She is supposed to be peeling apples but the apple lies half uncoiled in her lap. Her eyes have a film over them like the glassy sea in Revelation. When she notices me looking, the film slides away and she smiles, but the film comes back. She is like one of the hollow crayfish I see in the stream, but I can't save her because I don't know what is sucking her dry and making her empty. I can't set her free. You can do that,

God, but for some reason You are not. God, why are You
punishing us if You come to me? Perhaps it is not You
who comes to me. I thought it was, but now I'm not sure.

About four o'clock we heard the crackle of tyres in the
courtyard. My mother jumped up, turned the grill down
to one and put the kettle on.

His face was dark when he came in. 'Anything to eat?'
my father said.

'Coming up.' She put the frying pan on the stove.

He pulled out a chair at the table. She said: 'How much
did you get for the dresser?'

'Two hundred.'

'The hallstand?'

'Seventy.'

'The tools?'

'About a hundred and fifty.'

'The mirror?'

'There!' He threw the receipt on the table and stabbed
the receipt with his finger.

She laid two pieces of bacon in the pan. He rubbed his
hand over his face. 'I did the best I could. That's it. There's
nothing else to sell.'

I saw her shoulders rise a little. She said quietly: 'You
know what I think about that . . .'

He looked at her as if she had slapped him. 'If you're
on about that car!'

She turned around and said in a low voice: 'You'd have
us live on thin air and that car sits there rusting!'

'I won't get anything for it!' he said.

'And whose fault is that?'

She turned back to the pan quickly and her voice was
thick and small like a child that's been disappointed and
about to cry. 'There's five hundred pounds tied up in that
car!'

He strode out and we heard the car start, the tyres ripping up the gravel, and she dropped into a chair by the grill and bowed her head, the spatula still in her hand.

I went and stood by her and after a while I touched her shoulder. She pressed her lips together and poked the bacon but for once she didn't speak to me. I went into the garden and leant against the pine tree.

2 November

Dear God,

Today the sky is as white as a fist. I can see the bones of the trees and the skeleton of leaves like wire mesh. Only the tall pine remains green.

I see now that summer was fooling us; it wasn't the truth. Green covered everything, heat made things hazy. Now I can see my breath, I can hear my steps, and there is nowhere to lie down and be covered over because everything is bare.

3 November

Dear God,

Mum can walk Elijah. She can cook. She can light the fire and change the beds and do the washing and peg it out. But she doesn't look right. She looks empty.

Today we went walking, her, me and Elijah. The sun was low and the land was sepia, like an old doily. I took the little camera, but she couldn't bear to have her photo taken and shielded her face. These late afternoons – when the trees and hedges are browning and the sun seems only a little higher than the earth, and the hedges and fields glow darkly as if they are burnished – give me a shifting feeling in my stomach. The bottom halves of things are lost in shadows, like a room in firelight, and the top halves – telegraph wires, twigs, the distant outline of hills – are raw and exposed, their tips pink and gold. The land is dead; it has stopped, and needs someone to wind it up again.

We spoke little while we were walking but I put my arm through hers. The only sounds were the gravel beneath our shoes and the scuffling scrape of Elijah's paws.

'Are you all right?' I said.

'Yes, darling,' she said.

'Only lately you seem sort of – tired again.' I didn't know which word to use. I said: 'Are you tired?'

She said she was fine, that she got a bit tired sometimes but she was fine. Then she looked at me and, for what seemed like the first time in weeks, really saw me. 'I hope you're not worrying about me.'

'No,' I said, and I smiled quickly at her, but suddenly I couldn't breathe. 'Just so long as you're okay.'

'I've never been better,' she said, and to begin with I was so relieved I thought I would cry, but then my stomach began churning again.

When we came back up the track she seemed thankful the walk was over; her movements were loose, she laughed at Elijah trying to get a leaf off his nose. But the feeling wore off when she realized we were home, and she became awkward and quiet again and her smile got stiff. Where does she want to be, then? Not here, and not somewhere else either.

4 November

Dear God,

Today they cut down the tall pine tree. I don't know how she held the chainsaw and didn't cry. I cried with rage. We have done something terrible. Already this place is not as we found it. The Tree of Life has been cut down. Or perhaps it is not the Tree of Life after all but *the Tree of Knowledge. But if that is the case, then what have we learnt?*

I step into the girl. 'Don't leave me,' I say.

The girl's heart is beating hard and slow. She knows she has to speak.

'Can't you cut one of the other trees down?' she says. The man's eyes are furious. It has to be that tree because it is too close to the house, he says, and it might fall in a storm. 'The tree is alive!' the girl says. But he isn't listening.

He shouts to the woman and she puts the saucepan of mince on the side of the stove and takes off her pinny. I see for the first time that he *likes* the woman watching him when he is angry; that if she were not there he might not be angry at all.

Elijah, the girl and I stand on the wall by the dairy and watch. The girl keeps her hand on Elijah's collar.

The chainsaw chugs into life and peters out. The man rips the cord again and again. As the motor catches, rooks reel away, cawing, into the still white air. Elijah flattens his ears. I don't know how my mother stands so close to the noise. I feel the first bite into the trunk. I see the tree shudder. He is wiggling the saw, bending it backwards and forwards in the wood. He doesn't need to do that.

His face is red, his mouth a gash. I loathe him. He roars louder than the chainsaw. The chain screams lower as it bites into the wood and higher as it comes away again. For a long time nothing seems to happen. Then the pine yawns, it tilts; there is a splintering sound and a crash, and when I look again there is great stillness and a space in the trees where the sky comes in. The girl did not look away at all. Now she is perfectly still except for her chest, which is rising and falling.

The woman holds the trunk while he cuts. Her face is red.

She sits on it, then wraps her arms around it, but whatever she does the tree still moves. He shouts: 'Hold it STEADY! Come ON!' I think perhaps he is mad. The closer the woman gets to the saw, the sicker I feel. Suddenly the girl is running down to them. He tells her to stand back. The girl's hands grip the knife inside her pocket and I feel its coldness.

For the rest of the day the sound the tree made when it fell stays in our heads and the stillness it leaves stays in the garden.

5 November

Dear God,

In the garden there are piles of stones that look like skulls; where there used to be trees there is sky; the earth is rent, we have exposed its insides. Of all the things we have done I think this is the worst.

Now there are gaps, places where the colour has vanished, holes in the ground and the earth and the sky. We have lifted off the colour and now see the bare paper beneath. Are we covering something over or revealing what was underneath? What was underneath was nothing: what we found underneath was white; in the stones of the ground, in the heart of trees, in the space where the trees stood. The heart of things is only whiteness. Inside the darkest hole, beneath the deepest root, it's there, gleaming. We scrape away, chisel back, burrow down – and we are blinded by light.

6 November

Dear God,

My mother is disappearing. She gazes at nothing, is silent, falls asleep. Each time she sleeps I feel sick and sit by her chair till she wakes. It's no good doing anything while she sleeps because I can't concentrate.

There was something wrong with my head today. The

sky was like steel and the wind seemed to have sand in it. I didn't want to go downstairs and find out how she was, so I made You come three times in bed, then took a sandwich and went down to the stream and separated thirty-five crayfish.

It doesn't seem to be doing any good, separating them, because each day there are just as many murderers as there are victims. I think I will have to keep on killing them for ever because they don't stop eating each other. The dam I made to keep the hollow crayfish away from the feeders isn't working either. Some of the shells have slipped and now there is just a waterfall. It occurred to me for the first time today that I might have it wrong: that maybe the crayfish are mating, not killing each other, or maybe they are ferrying sick relatives around like ants do. In which case I have been killing the heroes instead of the villains; in which case there were never any villains to kill at all.

This evening we read about Moses, how without blood it is impossible to be forgiven:

For when every commandment according to the law had been spoken by Moses to all the people, he took the blood of the young bulls and of the goats with water and scarlet wool and hyssop and sprinkled the book itself and all the people, saying: 'This is the blood of the covenant that God has laid in charge upon you,' and he sprinkled the tent and all the vessels of the public service likewise with the blood. Yes, nearly all things are cleansed with blood according to the Law, and unless blood is poured out no forgiveness takes place.

What have we done wrong, God? Why won't You forgive us? Even if You don't tell me I am going to keep writing to You. It is an act of faith. But it is also because I don't have anyone else to write to.

7 November

Dear God,

It is too cold to be outside now. The sky throws a strange light onto the land. It is gloomy, yet bright enough to make my eyes water. All day long the sun shines fiercely through a blanket of grey. It is like being underwater. Things feel as if they have been wound down so much that they have almost stopped.

This morning they cut down three more trees. He said the wood would last all winter. I didn't want to see the trees fall and took jam sandwiches down to the kennel. I made as many as I could when he was out bringing up the wood.

The sky was icy beyond the kennel door. A hard wind was blowing and there were little bits of hail in it. I ate the sandwiches and gave Elijah the crusts. I was going to make You come but in the end I didn't think even that would make me feel better, so I curled up in the hay with Elijah and listened to him chewing his bit of wood.

On the way back to the house I noticed that the mill-stone had split. I asked Mum if she had seen it. She came to look.

'Well, I never,' she said, 'it must have been the frost last night.'

After dinner I went and looked at the stone again. It had split in a straight line, right along the stain.

8 November

Dear God,

They are arguing again.

'You won't adapt!' she is saying.

'I'm doing my best!' he shouts back.

I am huddled beneath the blankets in my bed. I had my fingers in my ears but now I am writing.

I just heard my father say we would have to think about selling the farm. I thought of going back to the town and then my brain wouldn't let me think of it any more.

Please let us stay in this place. It is ours! You gave it to us, remember?

9 November

Dear God,

I had a dream last night. I saw a stone raised up in a high place. The place was flat, level with the sky. The sky was pale and white and so was the stone. The stone was stained red.

I remembered the dream when I was kneeling by the stream, killing crayfish. I was taking them from the pool and putting them on the stone. The blood was on my hands and the blood was on the stone. I separated the victim from the rider, released the victim, and took the rider's life. I did it again, and a third time, and then I sat back. I looked at the stone and I looked at the knife. I stood up and I felt dizzy. Suddenly it was obvious. Suddenly I knew what to do.

I don't know how long I stood there. Then I began to walk back to the house. I stumbled and got up again. Sweat was coming down from underneath my hair though the wind was cold.

Without Blood

Lucas is reading:

17 November

Dear God,
    I have waited a whole week and he still has not found work. I cannot do it again. Please let it be enough.

He frowns. 'What are we to make of that?'
I am silent.
He inhales. 'There is the drawing of the mouse, then this.'

18 November

Dear God,
    I can hear Dad snoring along the landing. The night is icy the other side of the pane. I couldn't eat dinner tonight. Mum thinks I have some sort of bug. I don't want to sleep in case I see the mouse again.

19 November

God –
    You heard me! Your law is perfect. Your law is true. He came into the kitchen whistling. He looked as if he had been running. He had found work on the other side of the river. He said: 'I knew it would turn up!' He had a bunch of flowers for Mum and fresh mussels. Mum's eyes filled. She cooked the mussels with wild garlic and butter and they laughed at dinner and her face looked like it used to. His was shining with cider.

Now I am in the long field. The air is cold as fire and the sky is blue. <u>I have saved them.</u> I cannot believe it. All around the land is full of colour, it is quiet and at ease. It has been wound and set ticking.

'What happened between this journal entry' – he turns the page – 'and this one? Why is the intervening page coloured with biro? – coloured so densely I can hardly see the paper.'

I consider Lucas, but am glad to say that he is not appearing in any strange guise today; he is behaving himself – or maybe it is my mind.

After our last session I asked myself whom I felt he was embodying so strangely, what I was 'projecting' – that's the word therapists like to use, isn't it? Though it seemed rather apt in this instance because, as I said, at that moment the room seemed to be nothing more than a shadow show or a film played on an old projector; there was something unreal, something of the replica about it. What I don't understand – if I was projecting an idea – is the fact that my antagonist, with whom I appeared to be engaged in a struggle, was cosmic; the figure godlike.

Do I see myself subconsciously as a god? If I do it is laughable, as most of the time I feel so powerless as to render myself meaningless. But 'project' has another meaning too, doesn't it? To forecast or predict. Does this suggest, then, that the weird epiphany heralds something to come? And then there is the fact that Lucas seemed to feel whatever I was feeling too . . .

'Well?'

'What?' I say, startled by his voice.

'What happened between this journal entry,' he holds up the xerox, 'and this one? Why is this page coloured in?'

'I don't know.'

We sit there for quite a long time, he eyeing me.

'Let's get you up on the couch.'

I lie down and begin to count backwards. My stomach is unsettled but I submit completely; there is no other way out. And the way out *isn't* out, as he reminds me; it's through. The problem is, I don't know how far there is still to go, or how bad it will get before we reach the other side.

'We're going to go back to that missing day, Madeline,' he is saying, 'we're going to recover what you were thinking when you drew the mouse. I'll be with you, you don't have to go back alone, but I can't lead the way, you have to do that . . .'

The room fades, the numbers descend and I am swimming through darkness. I sink down, down, down deeper still. The light moves above me. This time it is higher than I remember it being and when I hear the voice it is blurred. The voice says: 'Where are you, Madeline?'

It is a long time before I answer and when I do the voice doesn't sound like me. It sounds like the girl.

'In the barn,' the girl says.

'What are you doing?'

'Looking.'

'What's the barn like, Madeline?'

'Dark.'

'Tell me about that.'

'From the outside it's all you can see.'

'The dark is all you can see?'

'From the inside the world is white.'

'I don't understand.'

'The world is blind.'

A pause.

'Are you outside the barn or inside it, Madeline?'

'Yes.'

'Outside or inside the barn?'

'Inside.'

'What can you see?'

'At the corners, where the light falls, big weeds grow through the floor. Further away they are smaller.'

'What else can you see?'

'Streaks of red and brown, curved blades, big metal hoops. The light is shining through the little weeds by the door. The weeds are shaking. The sky is flying. The sky is frightened. It doesn't recognize me.'

'Are you . . . frightened, Madeline?'

'Things happened here. You can still hear the sounds.'

'In the barn?'

'There are things here but no names any more.'

'There are no words in the barn?'

I brush something away from my face.

'What are you doing now, Madeline?'

Silence.

'Do you like the barn, Madeline?'

'No . . . You can think things here.'

'What sort of things?'

'Sharp things. You can touch them too.'

'What do you mean?'

Silence.

'Tell me what else you can see, Madeline.'

'There's a trap.'

'What sort of trap?'

'A trap to catch mice in. My father takes them over the fields and lets them go.'

'Do you touch the trap?'

'Yes. And there is—'

'What?'

'Can't.'

'Can't what?'

A long way off someone groans.

'You're quite safe, Madeline. This is a safe place. Nothing is wrong here. Can you tell me what's happening?'

'The mouse is smaller . . . It is smaller than I thought.'

'Where is the mouse?'

A groan.

'It is brown and white. I pick up the trap and it runs round and round.'

'What do you do with the mouse, Madeline?'

'I take it to my mother. She is helping my father in the garden. I say I will take it down the field and let it out.'

'You're doing well, Madeline, this is important. Let's keep going. Where are you now?'

'I'm walking to the stream. Elijah is yapping at the mouse.'

'How do you feel?'

'The wind is blowing. It's like water. There is rain in it.'

'What do you feel, Madeline?'

'The sky is a shoal of fish. I am swimming with it.'

'But what are you feeling, Madeline?'

'The garden is watching. I am running from it.'

'But what do you *feel*, Madeline? Are you afraid, are you confused, are you angry?'

'The trees are creaking. They are bending. Their tops are swaying.'

'Don't you feel anything at all, Madeline?'

'Everything.'

'Everything?'

'I feel everything.'

A short silence.

'Where are you now?'

'At the stream. It has begun to rain. I can hear it in the trees. I look back but no one is following.'

'What are you doing?'

'I tell Elijah to wait at the edge of the trees. He whines but stays where he is. I go further into the trees and kneel by the stone.'

I hear the groaning again.

'Who is that?'

'It's all right, Madeline, it's no one. What are you doing now?'

'I have the knife.'

'Oh yes, I see.'

I wipe my face hard. 'I can feel the mouse in the cage.'

'Breathe slowly, Madeline. You're safe here. Nothing can hurt you.'

I shake my head fast. 'The mouse is stronger than me! How can such a little thing be so strong? The mouse is angry! I have to make myself angrier. I have to make my movements hard! I must be a machine! I set my jaw, I make my hands stone. The harder it scrabbles, the harder I make myself! I wish I could drown it, but there has to be blood.'

'Why, Madeline, why must there be blood?'

'It's the law.'

'Which law is that?'

Silence.

'What do you do next?'

'I take off my jumper. I open the trap and take the mouse in my jumper. It is lighter than air. It struggles, and then it doesn't. It wriggles frantically and then it is still. I am more scared than that mouse.'

'I know you're scared, Madeline. You're being very brave. What do you do with the mouse?'

'I press it onto the stone. I am pressing too tightly for it to move. I feel its heart beating. It is beating the world in and out. The whole world is beating in this mouse. The whole world is talking to me.'

There is humming in my ears, a hand on my shoulder. 'Breathe slowly, Madeline.'

'The mouse's eyes bulge. It makes a high-pitched noise. It sounds as if it's happy. The blade bites the stone with a gravelly sound. Something is running over my hand. *Get it off, get it off, get it off!*'

A scratch on my arm. 'Is that better?'

For some time I feel nothing but intense heat. I hear nothing but thudding in my ears. The vibration is so powerful my body seems to be moving backwards and forwards. Then it fades, I become cooler and I hear the voice again.

'There's nothing on your hands, Madeline. They're perfectly clean. You are being very brave, but we need to stay here a little longer, we can't come back yet. What can you see?'

'The head and body look like they did a minute ago. Except now one is there and one is here. I have made a space between them. This is not an animal any more. It is an object.'

I can hear wind in the trees overhead. I can smell vomit and soil.

The voice says: 'You can come back now. I'm going to begin counting and when I reach the number one you will regain consciousness.'

The numbers descend, the dark grows thinner, a prick of light appears.

I ascend and feel the waters part.

NUMBERS

*

Lethem Park Mental Infirmary
May 2010

Episode, 2.30 p.m.

Memory is a skating around or across, according to Emily Dickinson. If that is true, then last night I fell through. I sank. I have had an episode, the first for over a year. The whole thing took no more than fifteen minutes, but by the time it was over my clothes were clinging to me, and I could smell excrement. By that time Margaret and Steve were here but I didn't hear them come in and wasn't aware I was making any noise. They sedated me, bathed me and put me to bed.

Apparently I was violent, biting Steve and giving Margaret a nasty green bruise on her shin. She is in my room with me now and for the last three hours I have been slipping in and out of a treacle-ish stupor. I want to wake up because I keep dreaming, always the same dream. I am walking along the beach road. This time it is night. My clothes stick to me and my hands smell of blood. In waking moments I am nauseous and my muscles ache as if I have been beaten.

When I wake it is dark. I hear Margaret saying: 'I'm here, Madeline.' I want to ask her to help me sit up, but I keep falling back into a slumber. Then I am running through a land lit by moonlight that is rolling itself up behind me like a scroll, with something running beside me, making a shadow on the road, and I cannot outrun it, no matter how hard I try.

The next time I wake it is morning and I know I will be able to stay awake for at least a few hours and I will not need to be admitted to the sanatorium because I have stabilized. I can remain here in my room but will be under close surveillance for some days.

'How d'you feel?' Margaret says.

'A bit better.'

'I'm glad to hear that.' Margaret smiles at me but her face is grey.

My tongue is sluggish with drugs, but I manage to say, 'I'm sorry about your shin.'

'Oh, I've had worse than that,' she says. Then she looks at me apologetically. 'I have to go now, Madeline. Sue will be taking care of you . . . I'll see you Thursday. All right?' She closes her hand around my own, though Lucas has said the nurses aren't to touch us, and I look away so she won't see me cry.

As I listen to the sound of the door closing and her footsteps retreating down the corridor, I try not to think about the scroll or the road or the shadow; most of all, that shadow.

Holy Darts

It is raining at Lethem Park. We have heard the rushing all day in the horse-chestnut trees. It is like heavenly electricity, sparks from an anvil. I lie on my bed beneath the window and imagine the raindrops are darts, striking me over and over. Beyond the Platnauer Room are the sounds of the evening: a burble of voices, a wail that rises and ends abruptly, the banging of saucepans from the kitchens and hum of the hot-air vents. I hear a trolley passing through the double swing doors at the end of the corridor and the blow they deal the air as they swing to again. Behind all these things is the sound of the rain amongst the newly green trees and shady walkways, finding its way into each creased leaf, each crevice of bark, into the dark, open-mouthed soil. There is something intimate about rainfall. It is as if an invitation has been extended to experience the earth on more intimate terms, to descend into the bowels of a ship, be shown the workings. 'Step into my parlour,' says the rain.

The window of the Platnauer Room is open a little this evening when I visit Lucas and I can smell the rain, and with it earth and bark and leaves. I am glad, it makes me feel calmer. Nevertheless, my voice still shakes with anger.

'It was too much,' I say to Lucas. 'Whatever we did or didn't do last time.'

'I think you did extremely well, Madeline,' he says.

He looks at me darkly, his expression somewhere between deepest sympathy and deepest cunning, and a wave of blood sweeps along my jaw and scalp.

'Therapy must be challenging, Madeline, or there is no point undertaking it. I want to assure you again that though what we're doing feels extremely difficult to you, it's just such difficult experiences that make me certain we are on the right track; when things are going smoothly it means we are stationary. What we must *not* do now is slow the pace; the way out is through. But you're right: we need to talk about what happened yesterday; despite what you think, I am concerned. This hasn't happened for over a year, is that right?'

'Yes.'

'Do you think our last session was what triggered it?'

'Yes.' My heart is beating so hard that I swallow, pulling my collar away from my neck.

'How much of it do you remember?'

'I remember blood, on my hands. I remember the woods and the rock.'

'It was without doubt the most illuminating session yet.'

I close my eyes. I cannot stomach the suit today, the aftershave, the lustrous hair, this creature exuding health, wealth and impregnability.

'What are your feelings about what we uncovered, Madeline?'

'I don't have any,' I say.

'But you had an episode.'

'Apparently.'

'You have described the sensation during your last episode as like being engulfed in a white cloud,' he says; 'at least, that is what is written in the notes here. Does it still feel like that?'

'It feels like being wiped out,' I say quietly.

He watches me. 'Eliminated?'

'No. Erased.'

'I see . . .'

He doesn't.

'You used the same expression when you were writing eulogistically about the first few months at the farm, do you remember? I think you used the word in reference to sunlight, then later to describe how it felt when God "came" to you.'

He looks at me for a long time but, since there is nothing forthcoming, returns to his notes.

'There is only one other picture in the journal: the dead bird. Am I to take it this was an "offering" too?'

The word sounds patronizing on his tongue: archaic, foolish.

I do not answer. I listen to the rain.

'What happened in the months leading up to this entry?'

When I feel calm enough I open my eyes. 'My father couldn't find work.'

'What was the reason this time?'

'The same as before: the islanders excluded him.'

'I thought I read that he did find work?'

'For a short time,' I say, 'but it didn't last. He came home drained. My mother said he had been having a hard time with the men. One told him to do something one way, another told him something different. We were very poor.' I listen to the rain. 'It rained a lot too. It was the wettest year on record. It rained for two hundred and thirty-one days,' I say. 'And there were other things. There was the chimney.'

'What happened to that?'

'Lightning struck it.' I look at him. 'And there was the fire.'

'Fire?'

'In the roof. And the flood because the plumber fused the electrics.'

'A whole catalogue of disasters.'

'And there was no end to the stones in the ground. Nothing could be done with it. But the worst thing was the rain.'

'Would you tell me about that?'

I inhale and breathe out very slowly. 'It rained at the island for two hundred and thirty-one days,' I say. 'My father made notches on the dairy wall. The stream became a cataract, the garden was full of the sound of water. All day mist and cloud hid the mountains; when you entered a room it was like going into an underwater cave. My mother said it was like Doomsday.'

'Your father took the opportunity to make alterations to the house,' he says. 'You've written for 10 February:

All day rain wraps us in grey blankets. The house is filled with rubble and the sharp tang of dust. They took the rotten skirting board off the walls and burnt it in the courtyard. He ripped out the cupboards around the fire with a crowbar and a sledgehammer and it echoed in the fields. When I came out he was hacking plaster from the kitchen walls and began brushing the cracks. Mum swept up. As often as she had made a clean space he dislodged more chunks. Then he ripped the sweeping brush from her and pounded the walls with it. Avalanches of grey powder fell to the ground.

I went and sat with Elijah in the kennel. Rain was coming down so fast it looked as if there were sparks coming off the cobbles. When I came back he was repointing the walls, sweat running down his face. The trowel made a sound like broken glass. He lunged at the wall again and again. Mum was bagging rubble and the skin of her face was taut.

He looks up. 'The pen presses so hard in one place, you've gone through to the next page.'

He looks at me, then begins to read the next entry.

11 February

When he came home from town today he started ripping the lino up. Mum was cooking dinner. She said: 'Can't it wait?' but he said: 'No time like the present!' and wrenched even harder. The lino was stuck to the tiles with something sticky, it looked like tar.

They made a fire of it when the rain stopped. The yard was full of black smoke. The lino wouldn't burn . . .

He goes on: 'You've copied out a verse from the bible.'

When you come into the land of Ca'naan, which I am giving you as a possession, and I do put the plague of leprosy in a house of the land of your possession . . . they must clear out the house before the priest may come in . . . and they must tear out the stones in which the plague is.

'There's another verse on the' – he turns back – '17th.'

And if the plague has spread in the house, it is malignant leprosy in the house. It is unclean. And he must have the house pulled down with its stones and its timbers and all the clay mortar of the house and must have it carried forth outside the city to an unclean place.

He looks up. 'Did you see the work your parents were doing as cleansing in some way?'

'I don't remember.' I hate the sound of my words on his tongue.

'Your mother is worrying you.'

Mum was sitting close to the woodstove with her eyes closed. Her face was grey and her hair was powdery and stiff. She looked like a little bird puffed up against the cold. She was holding a hot-water bottle that had gone cold. I made her tea and refilled the bottle. She said: 'Thank you, my love.'

He raises his eyebrows. 'And God keeps coming to you: "When God comes everything goes away. I need Him now. I did not need Him before." How did you make God "come" to you, Madeline? Were you imagining Him? Was this some sort of meditation?'

The rain falls more heavily suddenly, like a handful of chippings.

'I don't know,' I say. 'It was such a long time ago.'

'"*It is pain and ointment*",' he reads, '"*and while it lasts I am not here and I am no one. I was afraid to begin with but I'm not any more. I wish when You come You would stay longer. I wish You would stay for ever. But perhaps I couldn't live if You did. God, when You come it is so sweet! It is so sweet I think I am going to die of it.*" There's a whole literature written about just such experiences – Teresa of Ávila, for instance, pierced with the holy dart; Dame Julian of Norwich – have you read them?'

'Julian of Norwich,' I say. '"Smite upon that thick cloud of unknowing with a sharp dart of longing love." "Prepare yourself to wait in this darkness as long as you may." "It is none other than a sudden stirring . . . leaping up to God as a spark from the fire," "it alone destroys sin at its roots".'

A nameless woman in a cell in the fourteenth century, the world ravaged by violence, the Black Death wreaking havoc across Europe, dissidents burnt alive. I am tired of his interrogation. I say, suddenly: 'Where is Brendan?'

'What?' It is unlike Lucas to say something as undignified as 'what'; I must have startled him.

'Brendan.'

'Brendan is where he has always been.' His eyes glitter.

'On our ward?'

'Yes; haven't you seen him?'

'No,' I say. 'I haven't seen him for weeks.'

'Perhaps you and he have been missing one another.' There is the faintest suggestion of a smile on his lips.

I ask myself whether this is possible. I suppose I have not been to the lounge much myself recently. My anger subsides. I feel cold, and then profoundly tired. Does Lucas have an answer for everything, or do I keep overreacting and losing touch with reality?

'Our time is up,' he says. 'Keep reading the journal.'

When I get up, my body is slow and extraordinarily heavy. He returns to his papers and I go back up the corridor to these walls, lie beneath the window and listen to the rain, dissolving the world within and without.

Rain

1 March

It is raining. It has been raining for weeks. Dad is home all the time. Mum is tired. Elijah is bored because it is too wet to go out. God comes to me nearly every day now. I need Him more and more. While God is with me I don't think at all. I can't think. It is impossible.

2 March

I feel strange, numb. Is numb the right word? As if I am dreaming. To begin with, after I had done it, I felt sick. The sickness hung around like a smell. Then it faded.

I have been thinking about what is inside our bodies, what makes us up, how we seem to be just the same as an animal. Where does the life go? When we die what happens to us?

3 March

There is sticky stuff on the kitchen tiles. All day while Dad plastered the hall, Mum cleaned them in the barn but it won't come off. They can't get rid of the stuff of this place, it can't be chipped or washed or melted off.

Mum sat hunched over, bundled up in clothes. The cement froze as she worked. I brought her cups of tea and toast. Dad wouldn't stop and he made her feel guilty when she did. He wouldn't let me clean the tiles in case I broke any. I sat with Elijah in the kennel and put my face in his fur.

'Next summer we'll go to the beach,' I said. 'We didn't go this year. Next year, next summer, when it's nice and hot, we'll go to the beach, and we'll forget all of this ever happened.'

She cooked sausages and beans for dinner. He hates that sort of food. At the table I noticed her hands were still dirty. They were also covered in little cuts. Her hair was flattened and oily. He glared at her. Then he said suddenly: 'Don't you have a hairbrush?' My heart beat so fast then that I couldn't breathe. I wanted to hurt him a lot.

After I washed up Elijah and I went running in the dark. Our breath was hard, it tore at the air and our feet beat on the road. I could see the whites of Elijah's eyes. When we came back my legs were shaking. I didn't want to go into the house so I went into the garden. There was wind amongst the tall trees and the rhubarb leaves and the cold stink of cabbage.

God, let him find work again, if not for him for us.

4 March

Dear God,

This morning at breakfast he prayed to You to forgive us our sins and direct him to work, then went into town to look for more work. His shoulders were hunched up when he went off in the car, as if to protect himself. I suddenly saw my father as a child for the first time and I felt sick with sorrow for him. It is confusing when I stop hating him.

I began hating him all over again when he came home: he pulled down the kitchen ceiling and told Mum to get out of the way. To eat dinner we had to wipe the rubble and dust off the table. When I blew my nose tonight the tissue was black.

When we went to bed, a sea of rubble was covering

the floor. Elijah stood by the front door and just looked. I had to clamber over it to give him his food. He kept licking the empty bowl when he'd finished, pushing it around the cobbles, but I couldn't give him any more because there was no more to give.

The kitchen does not look like a room any more. It looks like a hole. I am not sure what my father is doing. He doesn't seem to want to remake things, just pull them down.

5 March

Last night lightning struck the chimney. All day in torrential rain he tried to put it up again but the fire still wouldn't draw and smoke was coming out of the windows.

This afternoon we went gathering wood on the mountain. Mum was very tired. We could see the island all around, the towns, the river, the bridge and the long golden beach we had passed last year, fringed with green firs. It didn't look that far away, perhaps a few miles.

'This summer we'll go there,' Mum said. 'Would you like that?'

'Yes,' I said.

6 March

Today a man came to do the plumbing. I was in my room reading when the lights went off and I heard my father shout: 'Hold it!' When I went down there was water running down the hall walls behind the fuse box and he was standing on a chair, ramming towels against the ceiling. The man came running downstairs, stared, then turned around and ran up again. After a minute the water stopped but the lights didn't come back on.

Tonight Dad was silent and sat by the woodstove, looking at his hands. The plastering in the hall is ruined, and the bathroom floor. He'd saved up to pay the plumber, and now the plumber has destroyed the electrics.

7 March

After dinner today the lights came on and he began skimming the ceiling. He made noises as if he was being hit or was hitting someone. Mum was tracing her eyebrow with her finger, over and over. Her eyebrows were raised and her eyes closed.

Suddenly he stopped making loud noises and made a small noise, like a child that has been hurt. When we turned he was standing below the lintel that ran over the woodstove, holding his head. A thin line of blood was trickling from it. Mum froze. Then she said: 'Al!' and ran to get a cloth. As she reached him, his knees gave way and he sat down on the milk crate. She put the cloth against his head and her hands were shaking.

I felt sick because I remembered I had wanted something bad to happen to him. Then I noticed that a crack ran from the lintel across the ceiling to the stairs in the corner. I felt cold, looking at that crack in the ceiling.

He couldn't eat dinner. His wrinkles showed white through the dust. But he sat at the table with us and he waited till we had finished, then said: 'Bible,' and I fetched it. He took the bandage away to read and I saw a cut in his head, with what looked like black jam inside.

The bible reading was about Achan, how one Israelite sinned and the whole nation suffered. We must have sinned again, because we are suffering. But which one of us has sinned? I don't think it can be me or God would not still come to me. But I am not sure.

10 March

Dear God,

The trees are misted in green, the earth is trickling and rushing, the land is being reborn but we are still locked in the cold. Why do You still come to me, God, yet punish us too?

We were sitting by the woodstove one evening that spring when we heard a roar as if a train were going over the house. My father went outside and came running back in. 'The chimney's on fire!' he said. When we got to the courtyard we saw orange sparks coming out of it, and flames. 'Fill them!' he said, and dumped two buckets on the pile of wet sand in the corner of the courtyard. My mother stood looking at them. 'FILL THEM!' he shouted.

He ran and balanced a ladder against the house and began climbing it. When he got level with the roof he crossed to the wooden ladder with the metal clasps that grips onto the ridge tiles. He went along the second ladder with his whole body pressed to the roof. When he reached the chimney he lifted the bucket with both arms and tipped it into the chimney. We had been staring at him, without thinking, but suddenly we both ran to the sand-heap and began filling more buckets.

'Bring them over!' he yelled.

I passed one to him at the bottom of the ladder and he ran up it, the ladder bouncing with each step. When he got to the roof he lay flat against the other ladder and climbed towards the chimney. My mother looked away. I saw him straddle the chimney and empty the bucket. He shouted down to us: 'Bring it up!'

My mother stared at him. 'Oh Al, I can't,' she said.

'I'll go—' I said. But they wouldn't let me.

He screamed: 'COME ON!' So she began climbing.

I stood on the bottom rung to stop the ladder moving but it hardly made any difference. The bucket swung and the ladder bounced. When she got to the guttering he grabbed the bucket and began to inch back up the roof.

'MORE!' he shouted.

I ran to fetch another bucket of wet sand and by the time she was at the bottom of the ladder I had it ready to hand to her. Her face was red and her eyes were staring. She said: 'Thank you, my love,' and went up again. She was going slowly, looking where she put her feet.

He screamed: 'COME ON!' I closed my eyes and held the ladder so tightly that if it had been alive I would have killed it.

After a while there was no more smoke coming out of the chimney and he came down, his eyes enormous, his face blotched red and white, running with sweat. We went inside and my mother sat down with a bump. Her eyes were black and there were white rings around them. I did not want to be around either of them any more and sat with Elijah in the kennel. He put his nose in my hand and I held it. It usually felt good to be close to him, but that night I could not feel a thing, only stared straight ahead.

17 March

Dear God,

Today while he was out looking for work Mum washed all the bed linen and all the curtains and all the cushion covers. When I came downstairs a bit later I found her treading her clothes in the bath with only her pants on.

'Are you all right?' I said. I did not like to look at her too directly.

'Yes, why?' she panted.

I couldn't think of a reply.

We hung it all on the line, then I played catch with Elijah in the courtyard. When I came in she was clothed and asleep by the cooker. Her head was back and her mouth open.

When he got home his eyes were dark. He looked at Mum, then at me, and we were both embarrassed. I went outside again and he went into the front room. I think he was frightened.

Dear God,

    There was mist this morning. The sun didn't come until noon and then quickly slipped behind the hills. We went shopping in town. We drove very slowly on half throttle and at the garage put one pound's worth of petrol in. Dad wasn't sure if it would get us there. Mum was crying. I was saying silently over and over: Help us, please help us.

    Perhaps You heard me; coming home, we found coal in the road.

I remember one afternoon that spring I had a stomach pain and my mother sat with me and gave me paracetemol. 'Can you stay here if I go to sleep?' I said, and she said she would. She put her hand on my forehead and almost looked like her old self again. The unsleepy self, the self that wasn't frightened of everything, the self that was like a grown-up.

When I woke it was evening and she had gone. Down below in the courtyard I could hear a short rasping noise. It was lighter than it had been for a long time, the rain had stopped and the sky was clear. I went to the window and looked down. My father was wheeling a barrow of turf. I asked him where my mother was.

'Eh?' he said, in the infuriating way he had of pretending not to hear, and I repeated the question.

'She went for a walk!'

My heart beat hard. 'How long ago?'

'*I* don't know!'

The cuts of his spade rang in the air again. I pulled on my jeans and ran downstairs. Outside, the air was warmer than it had been, almost balmy. I could smell the earth and the vegetation, and it frightened me. I began to cry as I ran down the track. By the time I reached the bottom and turned into the lane I was gasping and couldn't see properly.

Halfway down the lane I saw her and Elijah coming towards me. Elijah raced up, bending his body and groaning in happiness, then ran back to my mother, as if wanting to bring us together. I ran up to her and hugged her so hard.

She laughed and said: 'Anyone would think I'd been gone a fortnight.'

'Where did you go?' I said; I was taking in her eyes and her skin and her hair. I couldn't look enough at her.

'What's the matter?' she said, not smiling any more, wiping my face.

'I don't know—' I said. 'Are you okay?'

'Yes,' she said, and she looked deep into my eyes.

That was the problem: sometimes she seemed perfectly all right. For the rest of that evening I didn't leave her side.

28 March

God, she is sick again. I know it though no one has said. I heard him talking to her in the bedroom tonight. 'You have to make an effort,' he was saying. 'You've got to try.' My stomach was lurching. I got out of bed and knelt and prayed.

After a while I was just saying the same things over and over and no amount of hand-wringing made it feel any more real or any more powerful.

I got back into bed and put the pillow over my head and made You come to me. But You wouldn't.

This has never happened before.

29 March

She didn't come down to breakfast today. I asked Dad whether I could take her some but he said to let her rest. I asked if I could see her but he said she was sleeping. All morning I sat by the woodstove.

Please, God, by everything You have made, make things as they were. <u>Make her get well</u>.

30 March

Dear God,

In the afternoon we went to the doctor's, a small surgery outside the town. I had to stay in the waiting room and Elijah had to stay in the car. Dad was leading her by the arm when they came out. She was wearing her best pink jumper and she was very pale but she was smiling. She said: 'All right, my love?'

I snuggled up to her. I kept so close. I almost carried her to the car. 'What did the doctor do?' I said.

'He's given me some tablets,' she said. 'He says I'll feel better before too long.'

'Oh,' I said, and something leapt up inside me, like Elijah when he is happy, and it went on leaping all the way home. We went to a chemist and got tablets for her and I held her hand. Dad kept clearing his throat. Perhaps now he is sorry for having been horrible to her.

She was happy for the rest of that day, smiling, not tired at all; we made chocolate pudding and chocolate sauce. But the more I studied her, the more I saw bad signs: that she was smiling too hard and her eyes were too wide.

2 April

This morning we went into town to buy wallpaper to decorate the bedrooms. In the shop I began to feel ill; the lights were too bright, the music was painful, the world suddenly seemed to be like a nightmare, concentrated inside this wallpaper shop. I asked if I could go back to the car.

'Don't you want to choose the wallpaper for your room?' Mum said. It's a big deal because my father is paying for wallpaper. But I didn't want to choose it and I didn't care whether I have wallpaper or not.

On the way home I felt so sick I couldn't move or look at anything. Mum looked worried, and all through the bumps and the potholes and the cattle grids she kept her hand on my knee.

At home she sat on the side of my bed and rubbed my stomach. When I went to sleep she didn't go away. She sat there all afternoon. It was wonderful.

5 April

Dear God,

I wish she had never taken the new tablets. She comes into rooms and goes out again, she stares for hours into space, she sets lessons for me and can't mark the sums. She doesn't look at me in the same way. It is as if she doesn't know me.

This afternoon I went out to the field where the big pines grow. Rain was coming. The electric wire sang like the wind. I screamed at You and I shouted, but the sound was tiny and blew away.

It was not enough – what I did. You want more. I know now what I have to do.

The Bird

When I went under today I saw my mother.

She is standing at the kitchen window, sunlight in her hair. She is washing plates slowly, laying them to rest on the draining board as carefully as if they are sleeping children. Towards the end of our time at the farm she did everything in this new, careful way.

I stand beside her, wanting her to look at me, but she doesn't. She is smiling gently at something else. After we finish she says: 'Let me put on my trainers, kid, and we'll go for a walk.'

She goes upstairs, and when she doesn't come down again I go up and find her curled on the bed with her eyes closed. I can smell the acid of her breath and hear the 'pock, fff; pock, fff . . .' and I lie down beside her, and begin to cry.

The room is filled with shadows, those of leaves and trees passing over the ceiling with the strange, dream-like nature of daytime shadows; the second-hand, fabricated nature of them; seeming to move too boisterously, too theatrically, for the objects casting them. The garden is waking again, the sash is open a little. I can hear many birds singing.

I gaze at my mother for a long time. Her forehead is clammy and her hair smells sweet and meaty, coiled in oily slicks on her head. I gaze at her so long that my tears dry and I begin smiling – I smile so much that I think I might break into a laugh. I draw the blankets around her and kiss her once, very softly, in the middle of her head.

Then I hear a voice. The voice is saying: 'How did you catch it?'

The voice is a pain in my head. I rub my ear and burrow closer to my mother but it continues. 'How did you catch the bird, Madeline?'

It is as painful to answer the voice as waking from an exhausted sleep. And what is it talking about? What does it *want* from me? Why won't it leave me alone?

'The bird you drew in your journal.'

I look at my mother. I want her to wake because it is so rare to find her like this and for it to just be her and me. I want to wake her because I feel sure I will not see her again. But she is so tired – she is always so tired – and I don't have it in my heart to disturb her.

'Why are you crying, Madeline?' says the voice.

'Oh,' I whisper, and I am crying again. 'It's just my mother.'

'What is she doing?' The voice makes no attempt to speak quietly.

'She's sleeping!' I hiss.

'We can come back to your mother later, Madeline, but right now we need to find something out,' says the voice. 'We need to find out what you did with the bird you drew in your journal. Do you remember that, Madeline? Do you remember drawing it?'

'Yes! Can you be quiet?'

There is a pause, then the voice says, only slightly more quietly: 'Do you remember how you caught it?'

I wipe my face. I tell her: 'I'll come back soon, I promise. I know where to find you now.' My mother doesn't stir. She looks so peaceful. I am grateful for this but at the same time I want her to wake up so that I can say goodbye.

'Madeline,' the voice says. It will not give up. 'Tell me about the bird. Do you remember?'

I get up and tiptoe to the door but I can't go through it, and I stand with my head bowed.

'Do you remember how you caught the bird?' says the voice.

'It caught itself,' I say quietly.

'How did it do that?'

I inhale. 'In the bird-feeder.'

'Where was that?'

I take one more look at my mother, then go through the door and close it very softly. I am now standing on the landing at the back of the house, looking out of a sash window. 'In the garden,' I say, gazing down.

Beneath the window, the garden is buzzing and chirruping, greener than I ever remember it, and I see that the winter has passed and the garden is like it was in the picture in the bible. I remember the strange animals in the picture, and how each of them was a little human. And then I turn and see at the end of the landing what appears to be a large crow.

It comes walking down the corridor in its odd, wide-gaited fashion, its footsteps rasping on the wooden boards, and my blood feels cold. When it steps into the light cast by the window, however, I see it is not a crow but the doctor, with his hands behind his back and his black lucent hair and his black piercing eyes and his shiny blue suit.

'Why did you do it, Madeline?' he says.

I didn't do it; she did it – the girl, I mean to tell him, but perhaps he knows already. 'She had to,' I say.

'For forgiveness?'

'Yes.' I wipe my eyes and turn back to the window but I cannot see the garden any more for tears.

'How did she catch it?'

'She found it,' I say.

'Where?'

'In the bird-feeder. The top had come off and the seeds were far down. The bird was stuck, head first.'

'What did it look like?'

'It was speckled and dark. Very soft. Very beautiful.'

'What did she do then?'

'She went out to the garden and put the bird in her jumper. It wasn't difficult. The bird was too tired to do anything. She thought it might even have been sleeping. Then she worried that it was dead.'

'But it wasn't dead?'

'No. Just exhausted.'

'Where did you – where did she take it?'

'To the bottom of the garden. And she prayed it wouldn't die before she got there, because she had heard that birds' hearts are not very strong.'

'She took it to the stone by the stream?'

'Yes.'

'And she killed it?'

Yes.

She took the knife her father had given her, because she had pleased him, on an afternoon that seemed so long ago now, the knife with a red cross on the front. The bird was warm and weightless. She cut its throat. She lifted it and the head wobbled. The eyes were half closed.

The River

Wherever I am now, the girl is too. When it is quiet I hear her voice. We are no longer strangers. At night she comes closer, I feel her touch on my hair, she peers into my face, she is curious to see what she has turned into. In the morning I find her footsteps around my bed. It is good to have found her again. Others are pallid things beside her. She has come to help, knowing I am in trouble. She says she will show me what to do when the time comes.

'I am here,' I tell her. 'I am waiting.'

For the last week I have left my bed little. Margaret has been trying to tempt me with board and card games. She has taken to bringing in desserts on days when Carol is not cooking but I cannot eat them. So she has sat with me, knitting something small and white, looking up every now and then.

Unable to wake properly, I find myself wondering whether days are ending or beginning. My bed becomes a tiny raft, a woven casket. There is no part of it that I have not explored. I see the sun change position in the sky and the shadows slither sideways on the wall, then slip back underwater. It is surprising how often my thoughts come back to the same thing: that very soon now I will be home.

The girl and I wander. Sometimes we see somewhere we recognize. The girl and I go running. Wind chafes our ears, sun burns our cheeks, we run so fast the air hurts us inside. We go into the fields. Elijah is there. His coat is shining and he looks as he used to. I am so happy to see him. The sky is mottled and pearly, like a shoal of fish, the hour always noon. The fields lead down to a river. The girl and I stand on its banks. She seems to be asking me something but I do not know what. Soon, she says. Then the light swallows her up.

When I leave the girl I don't know where I am or sometimes how long I have been away; today I asked Margaret whether I was thirty-two or thirty-three; yesterday I stood in the doorway of my room, wondering whether I had just been within or without; the day before that I do not remember at all, though apparently in the night I was groaning again.

'It's to be expected,' Lucas tells me. 'The present gets hazy as the past resurfaces.'

Margaret has interceded for me; for the moment Lucas has permitted me to stop the exercises. Now, most days, I ride up and down on waves of sleep. This afternoon I found myself walking down to the river. The fields were lost, washed pale in the evening sun, its light so low that the river was one long swathe of white, the swallows golden arrows in the air. The irises were smaller than I remembered, or perhaps I was bigger. They were happy to see me and I them. I slipped in where they grew thickest. The water and I are in love. We want only each other. I float, I dissolve, I am absolved, we become one. From the corner of my eye I think I see other eyes watching. But nothing can trouble me.

I see my mother standing on the bank. I call to her and she wades into the water. She smiles and comes towards me, her breaststroke clumsy, her head and shoulders juddering with the effort to keep afloat. Periodically her chin dips below the water, then by a process of great splashings she manages to raise herself an inch.

I swim under her and buoy her up. I try to show her how she can breathe easily and let the water bear her up, how she can bob for hours with hardly any movement at all – things

I have discovered here in my sleep. Then I become aware of the eyes a second time, gliding in and out of the irises, and I wish the creature or person would come closer; come closer, or disappear altogether.

'Let's get out,' I say, because I suddenly feel that the gaze of the thing is unclean.

She tries to swim with me but stays where she is. She clutches at me and her weight drags me under. She lets go and I come up choking, my nose burning. We try again, me alongside, half pulling, half pushing with one arm, but her body is too heavy and begins to sink. Her limbs thrash faster, she is spluttering.

She is drawing away from me – I think for a moment she wants to – and then I see that the current is taking her. I hold on to her and try to reach the bank but I am not strong enough. The eyes that were watching are larger now, the pupils dilated. Their avidity is horrifying; they seem to be feeding off our plight.

Things are happening fast now. The river is widening, there are woods either side of us, I see sand dunes. The sky clouds over and it begins to patter with rain.

I call: '*Hold on to me!*'

I try to swim towards the bank, but her arms are choking me, her body is heavy – astonishingly heavy, as if the world were condensed into her shape. I go under, I resurface. We try again but I am not strong enough. The current is getting faster, the bank retreating. I try to show her again that if she panics all is lost; I show her how to let the water bear her up, but it is no use, and the harder she struggles, the faster she sinks.

'It's just a dream,' Margaret says, when I wake weeping.

Evening sun, the gentle type that comes only in very early summer, slants through the window. The rain hung on so long, right through April and half of May, but now suddenly everything is different; we have had four days of brilliant sunshine and already I cannot remember how my room feels in a downpour.

'You shouldn't touch me,' I say.

'I know,' she says, but doesn't take her hand away.

After a few minutes she goes back to her chair and takes up her knitting again.

'Margaret,' I say. 'Can I ask you something?'

'Fire away.'

'It's a strange question.'

'All right,' she says, but I still don't ask her for quite a long time.

'Could you forgive someone for killing you if it was unintentional?' I say.

Her needles stop moving. 'What sort of question is that?'

I smile shakily. 'I told you it was strange.'

She puts the end of wool in her mouth to moisten it, then threads it through the needle, takes up one of the knitted pieces of clothing that are lying on her lap and places it edge to edge with another.

'Madeline, you're not meant to be thinking about this sort of stuff, you're supposed to be taking it easy.' She continues to line up the edges, then begins to sew the pieces together with loose yet perfectly measured stitches. She is frowning hard, as if I have greatly displeased her, but after a minute she says: 'Does this person know they killed me?'

I feel a surge of affection for her. 'Yes,' I say.

She stitches right the way down one side of one edge and realigns the next, and I watch the white thread loop and reappear as gracefully, as easily, as water beneath her hand.

'Then yes,' she says. 'I'd forgive them.'

There is a great heat in the room, between us and around us. It is difficult to think for the force of it.

'What if that person was your child?' I say, and my voice is breathy and barely there. She is very still for a second, then begins stitching again.

'Then it wouldn't matter whether they had meant to kill me or not; I'd forgive them anyway.'

I stare at her, then look away and close my eyes because I don't want to cry again. I hear her break the wool thread with her teeth and say: 'There!' She holds up the joined pieces and I see it is a small cardigan. It must be for someone's baby because Margaret doesn't have children of her own.

'It's lovely,' I say.

She looks at me, then lowers the knitting. She sighs as she gazes at me. 'You and your questions,' she says.

I nod – but at this moment I am happier than I have been for a long time. She has said she would forgive me; if it was unintentional, she would forgive me.

'We didn't mean it, did we?' I say to the girl, as I slip back into sleep.

She shakes her head. But then she turns away and for the rest of the evening I cannot make her look at me.

'And again your father found work?'

'Yes, a man came to the farm and said he needed work done on his farm. He didn't live far from us. He wanted a cowshed built, there were months of work, my father said. After all that time when my father went looking for work, it was right on our doorstep.'

'And things improved again?'

'Yes. Almost immediately. That night, I thought my mother would get better. She sat by the fire and stroked my hair and seemed like herself again. That night, for the first time I slept all the way through. After that she stopped taking the new tablets.'

Dr Lucas puts down his pencil. 'Madeline, the material we've uncovered presents us with a bit of a problem. The final fugue is becoming more and more out of character: you consistently chose to act, not to run away from the situation, this time to the detriment of your health. For example,' he picks up the journal: '"*I have bad dreams. I have seen yellow eyes. I have seen an animal in the middle of the night get up from the chair and lean over my bed. I do not know what he wants.*"'

'That sounds pretty disturbing. Do you remember this dream?'

'No.'

'Do you still have it?'

'No.'

'And this, for example: "*I am waiting. I wait in the fields, in the house and in the garden. I wait in the lanes and in the fields. Hear me. Save us again.*" You believed your father finding work was a result of God hearing your prayer?'

'Yes.'

'You still believe it?'

'Oh, no; I did then.'

'And how long did God's "help" last?'

'Till early summer, the beginning of June.'

'How can you be so exact?'

I flush.

'Wasn't it only a week or two later that you found your mother?'

'I need to lie down,' I say.

And he lets me.

The Curse

It is easy to offer a life up but not so easy to return it. The first man lost life for humankind, and the second gave it back, though at the last moment he famously asked: 'Lord, Lord, why have you forsaken me?' A sign, if one was needed, that not all offerings are accepted, not all bargains honoured.

We lost our bargain with God one day in June. Each day that summer the sky was clear in the morning but by afternoon great masses of sulphurous cloud had built up and the sun was no more than a brassy haze. I began to think the earth held some sort of badness that rose with the heat and clouded the sky like steam on a window. There wasn't a breath of air. Flies buzzed, died and piled up at the windows.

My father worked at Skinner's farm every day. He came home with pickles from Mrs Skinner or wine from Mr Skinner and tales of his charismatic employer. At dinner my parents began to talk about making a tearoom in the dairy again, about renting the barns as holiday cottages. My mother wallpapered and painted while I sat and watched or pasted sheets for her. It was good to smell the paint and glue, to see the rooms transformed after so many months of darkness into airy chambers.

But I felt leaden, weighed down with something or other. My nose bled every day that summer and I got tired of leaning over the basin to let it drip, so I began swallowing the warm, meaty clots. I wasn't hungry or thirsty, I wasn't sleeping much either. From the vantage point of the earth, a person poised on the edge of a black hole would appear to remain there indefinitely, whereas from the vantage point of the black hole, he would be swallowed up instantly. Apparently at some level, time, as we are accustomed to think of it, does not exist and we live in an eternal present; of all the days of our year at the farm, the afternoon we lost God is the clearest, as if it were happening still.

There was a pain at the base of my stomach that morning that made me sweat. My mother gave me indigestion tablets but they didn't work. She was going through old rolls of wallpaper upstairs, seeing which lengths would do for the end bedroom. I was drinking water at the kitchen sink, trying to take away the pink chalky taste of Gaviscon. Beyond the window I could see cows lying down in the field. I watched them tumble heavily to their knees, then fold their legs up. I watched their mouths moving slowly in circles. My hands shook, my eyes were muzzy and my legs weighted down as if the blood had coagulated there. I didn't know what was the matter with me. I got up and went into the garden.

I went down through the grass to the apple trees. I could feel the garden's eyes. I knelt, then lay in the grass. I curled around the pain and tried to comfort it; when that failed I tried to smother it, but I couldn't. I began to move my legs back and forth. The pain grew greater, the sun more piercing, the kaleidoscope of light and shade above me more dazzling. Sweat slipped down my spine. The pain became so intense that I began to pray. Then I put my hand between my legs, and I made God come to me.

The pain spoke this tongue; it grew greater for a minute, then began to subside. I curled up more tightly, blocking out thought and sound and sight. The pleasure mounted, suddenly flowed over – and for a moment the pain went away and I was nowhere.

'Madeline—' She was standing over me.

I scrambled to my feet, my face burning. I thought I would vomit and I didn't know why. Her expression frightened me. She was afraid – of me or what I had done, I didn't know. But as suddenly as the horror appeared on my mother's face, it vanished.

She said: 'My love – you've got your period.'

I looked down. My hands were bloody. My heart beat hard and infinitely slowly. I stared at my hands as if they did not belong to me.

'I didn't know,' I said.

I don't know why I said it or what I referred to. I could hear crickets in the grass. I looked up. I felt as if I were pleading with her, racing towards her, trying to reach her before something happened – I didn't know what, or even whether it already had; I felt I must reach her but I was too late.

'Let's get you cleaned up,' she said, and we walked back to the house. I don't remember thinking anything but it was as if I was falling, as if the world I knew was rending a little more with each step.

She was very kind. She sat me on the side of the bath. She took my dirty clothes, fetched clean ones, painkillers. But she did not touch me and her smile was firm. There was a stillness between us; it filled the little bathroom to bursting. Each movement was painful. I kept trying to get a glance at her face but she wouldn't look back at me. She had never avoided my gaze before; and she had never *tried* to be kind to me.

'It's all right, isn't it?' I said. I sounded slightly insane. 'Everything seems different!'

'Of course it's all right.'

She smiled again, but I began to cry and threw my arms around her waist. 'I was going to tell you!' I said. I buried my face in her stomach. 'I can make God come to me.'

She felt stiff and cold. She took my arms from her waist and smiled the new smile, level and firm. She said nothing about God, only: 'Let's get you a hot-water bottle. It helps the aching.'

The pain wasn't bothering me any more. I began to sob uncontrollably, the sound ugly, absurd. 'Don't tell him!' I said.

She knew who I referred to; she said she would not. She spoke in a low voice. She said once again: 'Let's get you a hot-water bottle.'

She settled me in bed and smiled at me in that new way again and I wanted to run after her when she went out. I curled on my side and sobbed till I slept.

When I woke it was night and the pain made me writhe. I slipped back into a fitful sleep in which I continually dragged resistant clothes onto my wet limbs though when I looked down I was still naked. I woke and lay panting in the darkness. There was no longer any room for doubt: I had found not God, but sin. Possibly the very sin my father had warned about. Uncleanness, immorality, unnatural desire. The root of it all.

I got out of bed and knelt on the floor. '*Forgive me.*' I buried my face in the blankets. I screwed my eyes up. I wrung my hands till they shook. '*Forgive me. I didn't know.*'

Or *had* I? Why had I jumped up when my mother found me, as if she had caught me red-handed? Why had I never told her about God's visitations? Was it simply because she would not have believed me?

Yes, came the answer. *Yes, yes!* But I could not trust it.

Another day began. The sun went on shining, the cows went on chewing. Birds went their way, leaves shimmered, fields were awash with insects and grass. Another day began – and it did not.

Synchronicity

Resistance perpetuates that which is resisted. If blood is shed, sin, so the law says, can be forgiven. But shedding blood is itself a sin – and a memorial; an act of worship to the god who made sin, a covenant to time indefinite between humans and gods and that which is higher than them, that says: 'This is important. Remember this.'

Memory is a burden synonymous with sin, a coming again and a judgment. Atonement cannot help but replicate itself, a snake with its tail in its mouth, and recreate the past in the present. But forgetting is erasure, a rupture. If sin was not remembered there would be no need of redemption – so it must be, by flames and incense and prayer and blood. And without time there would be no remembrance, and no forgetting. The two things are one, the heel and the head, pleasure and pain, kernel and husk; the incarnation of God as man the same as a god dying in place of man; to be forgiven only to be condemned, to be forgiven again. So the pendulum swings. There is no redemption as long as there is remembering, no release but repetition, no end but addition. The law is simple, though there are different ways of expressing it. But sometimes it is impossible not to rail against it, not to try to step out of the circle, whatever the consequence.

It is only gradually that I realize Brendan will not be returning to us. I don't think Margaret or any of the nurses know any more than me. I am sure that is the way Lucas wants it; he will keep the final decision secret till the end. I don't know what he has done to Brendan but I know it is Lucas who has had him taken away. I ask Margaret whether Brendan is in Block 'H' but she says she doesn't know. I know it is Lucas who has made Brendan disappear because it is Lucas who has been shamed by Brendan's behaviour. And so he sent a message: disobedience will not be tolerated. Eye will be for eye, tooth for tooth, life for life.

'Brendan needed some time alone,' Lucas tells me today when I ask him.

'But where is he?'

'Somewhere where he can best be cared for.'

'What does that mean?'

He doesn't answer.

'Can I see him?'

'No. Not at the moment.'

'Will I see him again?'

'I don't know, Madeline; that depends on the trajectory of both your treatments.'

I stare at Lucas. Will it work – his magnificent regime? Will he really succeed where others have failed? Or will he be beaten by the sheer weight of our imperfection, our inveterate helplessness?

'You're still resisting,' Lucas says to change the subject. 'What is this sin that's too terrible to talk about, Madeline? You know it will come out under hypnosis.'

'Yes,' I say, 'so it doesn't matter if I don't talk about it.'

But I am not thinking of the doctor any longer but of the girl. I have not seen her for three nights. It is unbearable to lose her so soon after finding her again.

'You demonstrate a remarkable ability to believe that you influenced the course of events,' he is saying, 'acting out some redemption allegory in which ordinary incidents became extraordinary and are studied for their greater significance – in this case God's assumed disapproval. This isn't uncommon in dissociative amnesia: the individual believes he can make things happen, create change, cause thought and reality to conjoin; it's called synchronicity. The cause and effect relationship is sometimes immediate, sometimes delayed, but nevertheless assumed to be connected because the events themselves may be unusual. In your case your religion provided a fertile ground for such imaginings because, as things turned out, they seemed to corroborate your world-view: God listening, punishing, rewarding, exempting from punishment. But you give significance only to that which reinforces your theory, Madeline; that's why you need to share your memories, air them. Now I am going to ask you again what you remember about your mother's death. Perhaps it will help to talk about the days leading up to it.'

I look at my hands for some moments. I say: 'I was coming downstairs, my mother was crying, my father was standing at the table holding a piece of paper – a letter.' And I see him again, standing so still.

'Who was the letter from?'

'Mr Skinner. It said that the job my father had done was shoddy. It said a fair day's work for a fair day's wages. My father said he'd done a good job; he always did a good job. And it was true: my father was the best worker.'

'Did your father get the money that was owed to him?'

'No.'

'Wasn't there a contract?'

'No, just an agreement.'

'Wasn't he paid in instalments?'

'Yes. We got the first one, I think, but that was all.'

'It makes me sick,' my father said, and then he was quiet, and I sat down on the stairs as if I had been winded. It was unlike him to refer to his feelings in any way.

He went through the front door, saying he was going to knock Skinner's wall down, and my mother ran after him and put her arms around him. I saw my father's face over my mother's shoulder and it was horrifying.

He got into the car and my mother begged him not to go. But he said it stuck in his throat: that all the scrimping and saving, all the hours wondering where the next job was coming from, trying to get the place finished on a shoestring, was nothing in comparison with this. The car roared down the drive.

My mother came back to the house. Her feet made a sluggish sound on the stones. I noticed she wasn't wearing a bra. I suddenly saw how she would look as an old woman. She went to the table and put her head in her arms and I stood beside her.

'Mum,' I said. I began to cry. 'It's my fault.' It terrified me that she didn't look up.

The Stranger

4 *June*

God in heaven,
  Forgive me. Forgive me. I didn't know what I did.

9 *June*

Dear God,
  I asked her this morning: 'Are we really going to have to move?'
  She said: 'I don't know.'
  Please don't take the farm from us. Please punish just me instead.

10 *June*

Dear God,
  Her voice is thicker, her movements heavier. She looks at me as if she has never seen me before, as if I were a stranger, and I cannot bear it. I do not want to know whether she still loves me or not.

11 *June*

Dear God,
  He has put the farm up for sale and taken more things into town to be sold. She sleeps all day in bed. I have done this to her. I have done this to us all. It was me all along. You and I alone know this.
  I sat in the kennel. Elijah licked my hands and face.

Perhaps he knew it was me. Perhaps he knew all along and that was why he was afraid.

When I woke he was watching me. He watched me all the time I slept, I reckon. Then he butted my hand and we went back up to the house with him close to my side.

Elijah still loves me. Perhaps he is the only one. He will always love me, no matter what I have done. Until I die, or he does.

The Serum

Lucas is flicking something, tapping it with his finger. I turn my head and see a needle.

'It will ease facilitation,' he says. 'At this point it's necessary, Madeline. We're so close but you keep sheering away. It will make things easier, I promise.'

I open my mouth but he is already injecting me.

I can still see him and the Platnauer Room, though when I try to raise my head I cannot and everything is heavy and slow.

'It wasn't much more than a few days later that your mother took the fatal overdose, is that right?' he says.

I nod.

'In your journal you say very little. What do you remember of those last days?'

I close my eyes.

'Madeline?'

I shake my head.

'Was it you who found her? I think it said in the notes—'

I don't know whether it is because I am drugged or because I am so tired but the doctor does not appear to me to be human any more but a machine. Machines are relentless.

'I found her on the bathroom floor,' I say without opening my eyes. There was a pool of vomit by her head.

'And you called your father?'

I nod.

He lowers the back of the couch and begins to move the light.

'I want to go back to that night, the night you found

your mother and she was taken to hospital. The night you ran away with Elijah. From three hundred. When you're ready.'

I take a very deep, very slow breath and attempt to follow the light with my eyes.

'Two hundred and ninety-nine . . . two hundred and ninety-eight . . . two hundred and ninety-seven . . . two hundred and ninety-six . . .'

I feel I am speaking through a mask. My eyelids get heavier, the world closes above my head, reappears, then closes once more. My eyelids kiss and become one.

I stand on the banks of the river. The field with white flowers lies behind me. I know that this time I will have to do more than dip my toe. I will have to go fully under. I wade out into the water, and this time I am alone, and it is into the dark.

Midnight

The house was feverish, the walls clammy, the windows empty-socketed. The moon shone through the branches of the apple trees. A smell of burnt grass and fermenting flowers came in through the open window.

'What time is it, Madeline?'

'Twelve o'clock.'

'Where are you?'

'My bedroom.'

'What are you doing?'

'I'm kneeling, talking to her.'

'To your mother?'

'Yes.'

'Isn't your mother in hospital?'

'Yes.'

'Then how are you talking to her?'

'In my head.'

'What are you saying to her?'

'I am telling her that I am going to save her.'

Only I could save her because only I knew why she was dying, and I knew it would have to be more this time; I knew the offering would have to be the first fruits; my best; because the transgression was severe, so were the consequences. To begin with, I couldn't think what I could give – and then I did. And when I did, I didn't move for the longest time.

I didn't think I could do it. And then I remembered Abraham and Isaac, how You saved Isaac, and I thought

You might do the same again. Then I thought I had ruined it by thinking that, and didn't let myself think again until I saw the sea.

I stood up and put in my pocket the knife Father had given me. I took off my trainers and went downstairs in my socks. I pressed my body against the front door so the key would turn smoothly and I stepped out. The courtyard was brilliant and the cobbles still warm. I put on my trainers and went down to the kennel and my legs felt as though they had lost their bones and become nothing but flesh.

Elijah jumped up when I let him out. He made groaning noises and grinned at me, bending from side to side. He must have thought I was going to take him for a walk. The moonlight caught his fur like oil on water and his eyes shone, and I knew suddenly that I was right, I would never find anything better, not if I searched my whole life. That here was my best.

I latched the kennel door and stroked his head. Then we went running down the track, with a smell of bindweed and thyme, a stitch in my side and the knife in my pocket, the blade turned inwards.

DEUTERONOMY

*

Lethem Park Mental Infirmary
May 2010

The Land's Edge

I don't know how long we ran but the moon was as bright as the sun and the air was white like fire all around me. It was like running through water, the moonlight dappling and flowing over everything, stroking my arms and legs, and everything seemed clearer than it had ever been before, the grass standing up white in the light and the shadows blacker than tar. Elijah's shadow moved beside me, passing over the land like a cloud, and his breath kept me company.

Sometimes I couldn't see the road for the light so I looked straight ahead, but my feet knew where they were taking me and whenever I began to think I closed my eyes and concentrated on not falling. The land fell away either side and the only sounds were my shoes and Elijah and me panting: heh, heh, heh; in, in, out. As we ran, it seemed to me the land was closing itself behind us, folding up like a book, and wherever we ran, there it was beneath our feet, but wherever we had been, there it was not; and I knew it was vanishing and would not come back.

We ran down to the bridge and along the river. The moon was making a pathway there, showing us the way to go, and we followed it. It was the largest, brightest moon I have ever seen, it blinded you if you looked straight at it, it was like a hole cut out of black cardboard and beyond it nothing but white light. We came to the Viking Settlement and turned left. I could hear Elijah panting and my own breath and the sounds of my shoes, but after a while the sounds disappeared and there was nothing to show I was running at all, and I didn't feel that I was, only floating.

Sometimes I would stop and when we stopped Elijah would put his ears up and look back at where we had come from with his eyes wide and darting.

After a while we came to a hill and sat down in the clearing at the top. The valley was brighter than daylight and I could see things that were a long way away. Elijah sat panting, his tongue flapping about in his mouth like a little flag, and he looked all around, the hairs above his eyes worrying this way and that. I put my hand on his head and he swallowed and started panting again and I couldn't look at him. We sat there, looking out at the land, and it was all right for a while but there was a tightness in my throat and soon I had to get up and start running again.

We went on, through villages where all the houses were sleeping and past fields where I could hear horses tearing off mouthfuls of grass, and the road and the fields and Elijah and I were more real than daytime and people ever had been, and so was the night. Little weeds and flowers stood up against the sky as clearly as if they had been cut out of paper and there were things too strange and too beautiful to speak of and I knew I was growing more this night than I had done all my life and was finally touching the stuff behind everything, as I'd tried to before, and the land was letting me now because it was leaving and in the morning it would be no more than a husk.

Abraham and Isaac travelled for three days; Elijah and I ran for one night. There was no desert and no mountain; the sea was close and that was the place God had shown me because the moon was shining on the water. We stopped twice more but Elijah wouldn't sit and stood looking back the way we had come, panting, and when he stopped panting he whined. I put my hand on him but he shook free and began whining again. Then I put my head in my arms and didn't let myself think about what I had to do, only that soon it would be over. There was a stile beside us and, in the field beyond, gorse bushes. A breeze was blowing over that field and I knew it came from the sea. We began to run over the field, but my arms were so heavy and my legs had pains in them and I had to run and walk and then run again.

There were no more roads then but I still knew where to go because the moon was pointing and God was pulling, and whether they were both the same at that moment I couldn't be sure. We came to grassland stretching to the horizon. The path was lined with stunted trees so I knew we were close to the sea. We followed the path and it led between hedges. Beyond was a field of colours – even in moonlight you could see them – small strokes of purple and pink, blue, turquoise and green, just like in the paintings by the Dutchman, and Elijah's hackles went up. I will never forget the smell of that field. It was thick and brown and beige and sickly, like the carcasses I saw at the sides of the road. But it was sweet too, as if death itself grew here and had just burst out of the soil before it entered something else. I saw how long our shadows had become. We followed the furrows and when I looked around at the little dashes of colour, they seemed to be writhing in the light. I don't know what grew in that field but halfway through it I began to run. I didn't stop till we got to the top of a hill but the smell was still with me.

This time when I got up Elijah didn't move. I patted him but he turned his head away. He was looking at me from the corner of his eyes, the little hairs above his eyebrows twitching this way and that, as if he was embarrassed by our proximity, as if he didn't know me and I had become someone else. Something clutched me and I pulled at his collar. 'Please,' I said, and began to cry, but he wouldn't move. I got up and began running down the hill and before

I had got to the bottom he was with me again, and we ran faster, we ate up the ground, straight to the sea, and didn't look back.

The land was flatter here, the trees were bushy and twisted, there was sand in the soil. In a few minutes more I heard it. We reached the road running straight along the bottom of the grass dunes that led into the pine forest and I saw the moon bigger than ever above the dunes, peering from torn layers of light and clouds like coloured paper, and the light was so bright that it flattened me and made me breathless.

I had forgotten how difficult sand was to walk through, or perhaps it was just this sand, this night. Elijah was behind me and wouldn't come closer and I no longer called to him. We reached the top of the dunes and saw the huge beast breathing beneath us – breaking, unbreaking; ending and beginning – and we went towards it.

I knelt on the sand and looked up at the sky. I suppose I was waiting for You to show Yourself. I was waiting for a sign. I listened but I did not hear a sound. I watched but I didn't see a thing. I listened and watched for ever so long. And so far I hadn't felt tired, but right then I did.

'*Where are You?*' I shouted. '*Come out!*'

And there was no answer.

A breeze picked up. Elijah felt it and stood restlessly. He was looking away, his ears close to his head, his tail between his legs, shifting from paw to paw as if they were hot, drawing up first one and then the other. I began to cry and I pulled him to me. He was trembling. I could see the whites of his eyes. I buried my face in his fur and my whole body shook. Then I parted the fur at his throat, took the knife and cut sideways.

He tottered backwards a little way and his hind legs folded. Then his front legs did too and he toppled onto his side, watching me, while the sand darkened around him. Then one eyelid drooped a little as if it was exhausted.

Above me I could see millions of stars in the gaps between clouds that were bruised and beautiful. Below me I could hear the sea's washing and heaving, washing and heaving, as if it could never be rid of itself.

When I looked back Elijah's mouth was slightly open as if he were savouring the air, but his eyes were glassy and did not see me. I picked him up and walked towards the sound of the sea. The waves kept pushing me back and I kept pushing forwards. I went in as deep as my shoulders, then began to swim out. When I could swim no more, I let him go.

When I got back to the beach, the first light was coming. I sat on the sand for a long time, then got up and began walking.

The Road through the Pine Trees

I am walking through pine trees, it is bright all around me. Pale mushrooms and ribbons of fungi sprout from tree trunks, the air is sweet and damp, the soil sandy beneath my shoes. Moonlight presses itself into the mossy clefts of roots, crawls into the tight whorls of night-time flowers—

—and right down in the hollows of the trees – in the roots and the cracks and the crannies, in each cleft and clump, in the coloured mosses and the ribbons of fungi and the bright beetles and bugs – there is light. And each blade and each leaf and each tree is illuminated.

Someone is moaning. The sound frightens me. I run deeper into the wood but a voice follows me. The voice says: 'You're coming back. You're coming back to the room, Madeline, you're regaining consciousness.'

Who is this person? How does he know my name? What room is he talking about? I don't want to come back to a room; I have to find my way to the road that runs through the wood, the road that will take me back to the farm. I *have* to find it.

'Madeline, can you hear me?'

I run faster, my breath catching and hurting inside.

'Madeline—'

The person is moaning again. It is an ugly sound. I wonder where this strange person is. I race faster, hurdling fallen trees, but the wood is thinning out, the sky is getting lighter, until they are both no more than gossamer, and I do not see a road but a shadow.

'You're coming up, you're waking, it is safe to wake up. On the count of three you will be back in the room.'

Grains shift before my eyes, I am moving through something heavy, heavier than the sand at my feet. I see a lamp-lit room, a figure at my side – a figure writing – a man.

He looks up: 'You've done so well, Madeline. So well. What a breakthrough.'

What is he talking about? Who is he? Where am I? I do not know this place. Then I look down and begin to shake: I do not know this body.

'Lie there as long as you need to,' the man says. 'We will be processing what you have uncovered, it's all going to be dealt with. I didn't anticipate these results – not at all! The issues that have surfaced will need considerable work, the dissociated material will need integrating.'

I sit up and topple off the couch.

'Steady!' the man says. 'What are you doing?'

I stand, swaying a little, staring at him. I can hear someone breathing so laboriously it sounds as though they are gasping. My body does not feel solid but gaseous.

'Madeline,' he says, frowning, 'why don't you sit down for a moment on the couch till you come to?'

He is about to take hold of me. I cast around for something and grab a yellow pencil from a nearby pot, a pencil that is sharpened to the finest of points.

'Madeline—'

He is coming for me, he is coming towards me. I must be ready. It is me or him.

I fall on him and he topples backwards, his eyes wide, his mouth open, holding his neck. There is blood on my hands and my face and my chest, and then blood on the desk and the wall and the floor, blood spurting in a wide arc, high above my head; it is so unexpected and so spectacular that I stumble away from it, staring. I do not notice the body in spasm below me, the thrashing legs, the scrabbling feet. When I look down he has stopped moving.

I look around. I must try to get out. I must try to find my way back to the wood. I run to the door and into a corridor. A person in overalls is coming along it. When they see me they drop the folder they were carrying and scream. There is shouting; I turn and begin to run the other way, but before I have got to the corner someone is pulling me backwards, wrestling my arms behind my back, pressing me onto the floor. I feel a sharp scratch and my limbs relax.

The last thing I recall is travelling down a corridor that seems to go on for ever. I have to get back to the wood! I have to find the road! I must get home. But before I can call to mind why I must do any of this, my eyes close.

The girl wakes in a wood with earth damp beneath her cheek. There is sand in the earth and birds in the black boughs of trees. The sound falls from the trees and scatters itself amongst bushes. The sun is rising over the sea, winking and spinning itself out into skeins of light. It is going to be a hot day. At the edge of the trees there is a road that winds between pine trees. She gets up and begins walking.

EPILOGUE

*

The Long Corridor
July 2010

The New Doctor

I said that Block 'H' was the undiscovered country from whose bourn no traveller returns; I hope to be the exception to that, but cannot be sure. Time will tell. In any case, I can now tell you for certain that the end of the long corridor, instead of a singularity, instead of an end-point, is another corridor just like it and rooms just like others; I should have known it. There is one difference, though: the rooms here are padded, have barred windows and electronic locks. They are called Quiet Rooms. They are all right, I suppose, for a while.

I had another meeting with the new doctor today. Dr Hudson has taken over my care in the light of Dr Lucas's absence. She has a plan. If I follow it to the letter she says she anticipates results. Hudson's plan is called ECT – Electroconvulsive Therapy to be precise. It will help me, she says. Initially I had doubts. I remembered silly things I had read about ECT causing permanent brain damage, articles that said the overenthusiastic use of ECT had the same effect as a full-blown head injury. But these accounts are obviously unfounded; Dr Hudson says Electroconvulsive Therapy is an unfairly maligned, poorly understood and remarkably effective treatment for many intractable mental conditions.

'Intractable meaning "incurable"?' I said.

'Not "incurable"; "challenging",' she said. 'It's all about effort in here, Madeline, just like anywhere else. If you want things to change you've got to try new things out.'

I was not that convinced, but I respect Hudson; she is

the only one who dares to talk to me in person any more; the others do so by intercom, CCTV or through the grated window.

I did say, however: 'I tried to work with Dr Lucas.'

For a moment she looked at me with alarm. Then she blinked twice and said: 'I don't think it's appropriate to talk about Dr Lucas any more, Madeline.'

So now I do not.

The weather broke earlier this evening. I got up and stood by the window and watched the rain stand still in the forked lightning, and as I watched I could not help thinking about my new therapy. I do not know what ECT will entail, but at the moment I cannot be apprehensive. I cannot explain the peace I feel; I wonder whether Brendan also found that.

Here in the Quiet Room the events of my day are the changing hues of sunlight, the appearance of birds, the sensations on my skin. My sleep has become lighter, like waking; my waking deeper, like sleep; and, for some inexplicable reason, my body has been returned to me; its plethora of symptoms have miraculously subsided, and we are one. As with all good things, of course, my new health has come too late; now that I could easily walk to the lounge, now that I could be around my fellow patients without feeling in the slightest bit nauseous, I am not permitted to; now that I could fulfil Lucas's exercise regime to the letter, he is dead. Not that I miss any of these things very much.

The only thing that does sadden me is that I no longer see Margaret. She doesn't work here but came to visit a few days ago. I asked her to come in and sit with me but she just stood at the grate.

She said: 'I'm sorry, Madeline, not without someone here, I can't.' She looked frightened.

I said: 'I'm still the same person, Margaret.'

She smiled quickly and said: 'Of course you are.'

Then she told me she was looking after my things for me and that she thought it wouldn't be long before I could come back to the ward. She also said that she had heard good things about ECT and I should try to go along with Dr Hudson.

I said: 'I am sorry, Margaret,' and I meant it.

Her eyes filled then and it was a while before she spoke. Finally she said: 'You haven't hurt me, Madeline, you hurt yourself.'

'It was so good to see you, Margaret,' I said. 'Will you come back?'

She said that she would and she told me to take care of myself and not to give them any problems, and I promised I would not.

Going Out

Abraham went out without knowing where he was going. Many souls within these walls go out too, every day, without knowing their destination. May God, if He exists, guide them.

At four o'clock today I will have my first ECT treatment. I must admit that I started the day with a degree of trepidation but as it wore on the anxiety modulated into a gentle sense of grief. All in all it has been a strange afternoon; I feel I am packing and setting out again for a new country, like my father and my mother and I did all those years ago. A couple of hours ago I thought again of the day my mother and I first found the farm, how happy we were, and since then, all afternoon, things have been bursting into my head, little snippets I may never remember again – the night we chased the horses through the courtyard, preaching in the lanes on the long balmy mornings, the afternoons when Elijah and I lay in the grass. What happens to these moments if no one remembers them? Do they cease to exist?

The end of my journey is a room at the end of a corridor. At fourteen minutes to four I set out, escorted by a male nurse. We pass through double doors and beyond these find ourselves in a high room with an enormous white light in the ceiling. I have never seen anything as big or as bright as this light. I lie on a table beneath the white light and straps are attached to my arms and my legs. A woman with soft hands dabs my temples with what feels like water and gives me something to bite on. The water trickles into my hair like oil. I am an offering to the great white light. I trust the god will find me acceptable.

My heart is beating extremely quickly. I hope it will soon quieten. As they move around me, talking softly, I find I am standing on the banks of the river again. The fields of forgetfulness lie behind me and the evening sun is setting. It is at this moment that I wish Margaret were here.

But I am not alone: I look and see the girl standing beside me. I see her slim shins, the gold of her hair, the freckles on her nose.

'Don't leave me again,' I say to her, and she promises she won't. The girl takes my hand and looks back at the water. She is asking me something; I understand now, and nod.

We wait beneath the light, two human-shaped holes, with nothing beyond us but clear, shining space, and it strikes me now for the first time that there is something beautiful about these lacunae, about absence in general, an erasure so extreme. We are no more than openings – yet look what shines through us! We are 'not' – and yet we are infinite.

The girl closes her eyes. I follow her example. There will be words and there will be light. The words will blur and we will wander. We will go down a road, we will turn up a lane, we will round a corner. We will go further than we have ever gone before. We will see a line of trees, a track that looks familiar, a road sloping upwards. The trees will turn out to be those that we know. We will walk towards them. And sooner or later, one way or another, we will be home.

Acknowledgments

Thank you to Carole Welch, my fantastic editor, and to Celia Levett – the best copyeditor I have ever had. Thank you to Claire Gatzen for helpful suggestions and last-minute edits, and thank you to my agents Bill Hamilton and Rob Dinsdale – Bill for advancing advances and Rob for detailed and careful editing.

The Professor of Poetry

Grace McCleen

Elizabeth Stone has long been married to her work as a professor of poetry until, after a brush with cancer, she returns to the entrancing city where she was a student to research what she hopes will be her masterpiece.
But her surroundings transport her back to a time of loneliness and to an undeclared, overwhelming passion. When her rekindled friendship with Edward Hunt, her former tutor, begins to unravel, Elizabeth realises she is facing the biggest test of her life.

'Astonishing and luminous'
Hilary Mantel

'Moving and beautiful . . . a remarkable piece of work, empathetic, intelligent and genuinely poetic.'
Charlotte Moore, *Spectator*

'Incandescent . . . an intricate tapestry in which past and present mingle to mesmerising effect . . . and what eloquence! There are sentences here of such agile cleverness, charged with wit and beauty and enchantment.'
Hephzibah Anderson, *Observer*

'Grand tragedy with an intimate focus . . . McCleen's manipulation of suspense is extraordinary'
Beatrice Hodgkin, *Financial Times*

S

SCEPTRE